"KIRK, IF YOU AND YOUR FEDERATION DESTROYED THIS SYSTEM, YOU WILL PAY."

The Klingon captain moved a step closer to the camera so that his face filled the screen. "I will be watching."

With that, the screen went blank, then once again showed the destruction throughout the Tautee system. The rings were expanding slowly, the rocks and asteroids spreading in an ever-lengthening band that would eventually encircle the sun.

Kirk clenched a fist. It was time to get on with what they were here for. The Klingons could watch all they wanted, as long as they stayed out of the way.

"Mister Spock," Kirk said, "I need to know what's causing those subspace waves. And I need a way to rescue those survivors."

Spock glanced at him. "That will take some time, sir."

"We don't have time, Mister Spock." Kirk glanced at the destruction spread out in front of him. "And I doubt those survivors do, either."

Look for STAR TREK Fiction from Pocket Books

Star Trek: The Original Series

The Return
The Ashes of Eden
Federation
Sarek
Best Destiny
Shadows on the Sun
Probe
Prime Directive
The Lost Years
Star Trek VI: The Undiscovered Country
Star Trek V: The Final Frontier
Star Trek IV: The Voyage Home
Spock's World
Enterprise
Strangers from the Sky
Final Frontier

#1 Star Trek: The Motion Picture
#2 The Entropy Effect
#3 The Klingon Gambit
#4 The Covenant of the Crown
#5 The Prometheus Design
#6 The Abode of Life
#7 Star Trek II: The Wrath of Khan
#8 Black Fire
#9 Triangle
#10 Web of the Romulans
#11 Yesterday's Son
#12 Mutiny on the Enterprise
#13 The Wounded Sky
#14 The Trellisane Confrontation
#15 Corona
#16 The Final Reflection
#17 Star Trek III: The Search for Spock
#18 My Enemy, My Ally
#19 The Tears of the Singers
#20 The Vulcan Academy Murders
#21 Uhura's Song
#22 Shadow Lord
#23 Ishmael
#24 Killing Time
#25 Dwellers in the Crucible
#26 Pawns and Symbols
#27 Mindshadow
#28 Crisis on Centaurus
#29 Dreadnought!
#30 Demons
#31 Battlestations!

#32 Chain of Attack
#33 Deep Domain
#34 Dreams of the Raven
#35 The Romulan Way
#36 How Much for Just the Planet?
#37 Bloodthirst
#38 The IDIC Epidemic
#39 Time for Yesterday
#40 Timetrap
#41 The Three-Minute Universe
#42 Memory Prime
#43 The Final Nexus
#44 Vulcan's Glory
#45 Double, Double
#46 The Cry of the Onlies
#47 The Kobayashi Maru
#48 Rules of Engagement
#49 The Pandora Principle
#50 Doctor's Orders
#51 Enemy Unseen
#52 Home Is the Hunter
#53 Ghost Walker
#54 A Flag Full of Stars
#55 Renegade
#56 Legacy
#57 The Rift
#58 Face of Fire
#59 The Disinherited
#60 Ice Trap
#61 Sanctuary
#62 Death Count
#63 Shell Game
#64 The Starship Trap
#65 Windows on a Lost World
#66 From the Depths
#67 The Great Starship Race
#68 Firestorm
#69 The Patrian Transgression
#70 Traitor Winds
#71 Crossroad
#72 The Better Man
#73 Recovery
#74 The Fearful Summons
#75 First Frontier
#76 The Captain's Daughter
#77 Twilight's End
#78 The Rings of Tautee

Star Trek: The Next Generation

Star Trek Generations
All Good Things
Q-Squared
Dark Mirror
Descent
The Devil's Heart
Imzadi
Relics
Reunion
Unification
Metamorphosis
Vendetta
Encounter at Farpoint

#1 Ghost Ship
#2 The Peacekeepers
#3 The Children of Hamlin
#4 Survivors
#5 Strike Zone
#6 Power Hungry
#7 Masks
#8 The Captains' Honor
#9 A Call to Darkness
#10 A Rock and a Hard Place
#11 Gulliver's Fugitives
#12 Doomsday World
#13 The Eyes of the Beholders

#14 Exiles
#15 Fortune's Light
#16 Contamination
#17 Boogeymen
#18 Q-in-Law
#19 Perchance to Dream
#20 Spartacus
#21 Chains of Command
#22 Imbalance
#23 War Drums
#24 Nightshade
#25 Grounded
#26 The Romulan Prize
#27 Guises of the Mind
#28 Here There Be Dragons
#29 Sins of Commission
#30 Debtors' Planet
#31 Foreign Foes
#32 Requiem
#33 Balance of Power
#34 Blaze of Glory
#35 Romulan Stratagem
#36 Into the Nebula
#37 The Last Stand
#38 Dragon's Honor
#39 Rogue Saucer
#40 Possession

Star Trek: Deep Space Nine

Warped
The Search

#1 Emissary
#2 The Siege
#3 Bloodletter
#4 The Big Game
#5 Fallen Heroes
#6 Betrayal

#7 Warchild
#8 Antimatter
#9 Proud Helios
#10 Valhalla
#11 Devil in the Sky
#12 The Laertian Gamble
#13 Station Rage
#14 The Long Night

Star Trek: Voyager

#1 Caretaker
#2 The Escape
#3 Ragnarok
#4 Violations
#5 Incident at Arbuk
#6 The Murdered Sun
#7 Ghost of a Chance

STAR TREK®

THE RINGS OF TAUTEE

DEAN WESLEY SMITH
and
KRISTINE KATHRYN RUSCH

POCKET BOOKS

New York   London   Toronto   Sydney   Tokyo   Singapore

An *Original* Publication of POCKET BOOKS

POCKET BOOKS, a division of Simon & Schuster Inc.
1230 Avenue of the Americas, New York, NY 10020

This book is published by Pocket Books, a division of Simon & Schuster Inc., under exclusive license from Paramount Pictures.

ISBN: 0-671-00171-X

First Pocket Books printing May 1996

10 9 8 7 6 5 4 3 2 1

Printed in the U.S.A.

*This one is for
Len Wein & Christine Valada.*

THE RINGS OF TAUTEE

Chapter One

THE GAS GIANT THESAU, the ninth planet out from
the star Tautee, expanded, then contracted, as if it
were cookie dough in the hands of a huge, unseen
child.

Egg-shaped.

Then round.

Then oblong.

The large planet went through wild contortions
as it fought to somehow retain its shape.

And for a moment it seemed to have won the
fight, settling into the round, swirling clouded
shape it had had for millions of years.

Then the unseen child started pulling on it again
and the gas giant expanded at its poles, then
flattened almost as fast.

Every video screen throughout the entire system

was focused on those images. Millions of Tauteean people watched, awestruck at the incredible forces at work.

Half a kilometer below the surface of the second moon of the fifth planet, the entire staff of the Kanst Energy Center—thousands of researchers and scientists—watched their screens in growing dismay. Some people turned away. Others sat on regulation chairs, no longer able to stand. The remaining few stared at the screens as if the sight betrayed them.

In the center of the fifty-thousand-kilometer building, Subcommander Prescott stood in the middle of the war room, watching the screens. Her assistant Folle stood beside her. The rest of the room was empty. No one else cared to see destruction in three dimensions.

The war room was a round amphitheater, and she stood at the focal point, in the bottom, below all the workbenches, the computers, and the seats. The circular screens showed her the Tautee system as if she were on a ship in space. The system surrounded her and covered the ceiling above her. Only the shiny steel floor, which reflected the images in a blurry, colorful fashion, showed that she was in the middle of her creation.

The Kanst Energy Experiment.

She had hoped to provide unlimited power for all her people. The studies had taken most of her life. The research built on research that built on research, some of it generations old. She had hired ten thousand of the best minds in the system to work on the project. Their analysis, the computer charts, and the projections all showed success.

How could it have gone this wrong?

"It's going to break up," Folle said. "Just like Hancee did."

Hancee, the moon where the energy experiment had taken place. Where she had lost three hundred of the best minds in the system.

Prescott shook her head, the movement making her head ache. Pain shot through her jaw. She was grinding her teeth again. She had shattered a tooth when Hancee broke up, but her pain had seemed minor then compared with the loss of a moon and her people. Her friends.

Her pain felt even more minor now.

The amphitheater was strangely silent. She couldn't even hear the hum of the computers. The air was cold—the center fought a constant battle to keep the temperature steady within such a large space—and she wore only her thin lab uniform. Somewhere she had lost the extra sweater she kept for the cold days, the days when the cold ate through her thin skin, all the way to her bones.

That didn't matter either. She had a feeling she would lose more than a sweater before the week was out.

The gas giant's shape changes took place in that silence. She almost expected to hear rips and tears as the planet changed shape. The sounds of an earthquake, maybe, the grinding of shifting rock under the unseen forces.

The silence was eerie.

But the silence was better than the cries of dismay she had heard two days ago, when this room had been full of her staff, when all the scientists had gathered to watch their success on Hancee.

A success that had quickly turned into a disaster of untold proportions.

Hancee had been the largest moon orbiting the gas giant. Two days after they started the experiment inside Hancee, something had gone wrong. Nobody knew exactly what had happened. The project was generating the expected power, and the transmission beam was being put on line to bring the power into the population.

Suddenly the three hundred men and women on Hancee no longer communicated with the Kanst Center—or with anywhere else in the Tautee system. They were just gone, along with the power beam and the laboratories there.

Orbital photos showed nothing. The base was obscured by clouds of debris or gas. At least, her scientists thought it was debris or gas. It could have been anything, or something new created by the experiment. She had no way of knowing for sure.

She still didn't.

Two frantic days later, the rescue mission based out of the seventh planet finally received clearance to head for Hancee. It would have taken almost a week to get there, but the ships were still on the launchpad when the entire moon broke apart, scattering itself in small pieces in an expanding ring around the gas giant.

Now, less than a week later, the gas giant was

shattering, torn apart by forces she couldn't even imagine.

Prescott glanced over at Folle's strained and tired face. Somewhere in the last two days, he had stopped touching her, even casually, a squeeze of the shoulder, a brush on the wrist, all those soft unconscious signs of support. The others refused to meet her eyes, but the loss of Folle's trust hurt even more. He was her right hand, her best friend, her second-in-command, and her sometime lover.

And he blamed her for all of this.

Underneath it all, so did she.

Not only was she legally responsible—she set up the center, the team, and the research, and convinced the government the project would work—but she was morally responsible. She had believed in the project with all her might.

But no one could blame her for silencing the doomsayers. There had been none. Everyone thought the project would work.

Even Folle.

Prescott, her thin, tiny frame showing the wear of the last week, sank down into a chair and closed her eyes.

She had to think.

She so much wanted to believe that something else besides the project had caused this destruction, that some cosmic coincidence had led to this.

She might be able to make herself believe that the small forces they had been working with could destroy a moon. That remote possibility was the very reason the experiment had been placed so far out, away from the populated center of the system.

But the energy project couldn't have come close to generating even one-millionth of the force needed to tear apart a gas giant almost as big as their sun.

She hadn't caused this. She repeated the sentence over and over again. She hadn't caused this.

She hadn't caused this. It just wasn't possible.

But something was tearing apart the biggest planet in their solar system. And the destruction of the moon was damning evidence that her project had triggered something. What, she had no idea.

"You'd better watch this," Folle said.

She opened her eyes.

Folle was looking forward, at Thesau. The orange-and-yellow clouded planet filled the front screen. It seemed to have a large bubble forming on one side. As she watched, the bubble moved away from the center of the planet, pulling more and more of Thesau with it.

She stood. "This just can't be happening," she said to herself.

Folle placed his hand over hers.

She glanced at him in surprise. His anger seemed to be gone, replaced by resignation. He knew, as well as she did, what the bubble meant.

Strangely, it was his touch, his acceptance of the crisis, that nearly cracked her resolve. It was easier for her to watch when he blamed her. She could close it off, observe as a scientist instead of as a person.

Then he slipped his arm around her, strengthening her. She put her arm around him, hoping to give him strength in return. They would need it.

Because this was just the beginning.

She knew that now.

For the next hour they watched as the largest planet in their solar system spread out like jam on bread, forming the beginning of a huge ring that would someday, years and years in the future, fill the entire orbit around the sun.

The birth of the first Ring of Tautee.

There were fourteen more planets.

There would be fourteen more rings.

Chapter Two

Captain's log, Stardate 3871.6

The *Enterprise* has been ordered to the Tautee system to investigate waves of subspace interference coming from the area. Long-range scans have shown that some, if not all, of the planets of the Tautee system have broken apart. Admiral Hoffman believes that the Klingons might be involved in the system's destruction, although she doesn't rule out other causes. The Tautee system falls under the area covered by the Organian Peace Treaty, and the Klingons are looking for almost any reason to move into the disputed area. We have also heard rumors of the Klingons developing a new superweapon. My personal hope is that these rumors are false.

We have one other concern. A team surveyed the

Tautee system ten years ago, and found a space-traveling pre-warp culture insufficiently developed to have contact with the Federation. We are to arrive as quickly as we can, not just to stop any problems with the Klingons but also to see if the Tautee peoples were able to save themselves. Admiral Hoffman reminded me that the Prime Directive is in effect in all matters regarding the Tauteean people.

The *U.S.S. Farragut*, captained by Kelly Bogle, has been ordered to the Tautee system to give us backup if needed. Since I served with Kelly Bogle on the *Farragut*, this should prove to be an interesting reunion.

Captain Kirk tapped his captain's log off and surveyed the bridge. Sometimes, in the middle of long deep-space missions, the bridge seemed small and crowded. The padding in his captain's chair, usually comfortable, had grown thin. At Starbase 11, they would have fixed that, as well as done minor—albeit unnecessary—tune-ups to justify the *Enterprise*'s stay.

But Admiral Hoffman had canceled their routine maintenance. She knew that Scotty kept the ship in tip-top condition, and she also knew that the *Enterprise* hadn't been out as long as usual. Only the last mission had been hard, on Kirk as well as the crew, but had left the ship in good physical condition. He had looked forward to a stay on a starbase where he could eat food from someone else's kitchen, and have the days to read the antique real-paper copy of *One Hundred Years of*

Solitude that he had been saving for a special occasion.

Now it was beginning to look like he wouldn't even get one day of solitude. He had a hunch this mission would take as long as the last. Maybe even longer.

His mood seemed to be catching. The rest of the crew appeared to be just as disgruntled. Uhura leaned against the orange console, one booted leg extended, her elbow resting near the controls. Her long slender hand held her earpiece in place as she monitored the subspace communications, just as Kirk had requested.

Ensign Chekov looked as if he hadn't slept at all in the last week. His hair was tousled, and deep shadows had formed under his dark eyes. His fingers, tapping on the edge of the helm controls, provided the only real noise in the room.

Sulu was monitoring the navigation controls with a bit more interest than was necessary. Just before the orders came in for this mission, he had asked for time off to practice his swordplay. He had been planning to participate in a tournament scheduled on Starbase 11 during their stay. He hadn't shown obvious disappointment about the change in plans, but he did ask that his time off be canceled.

Only Spock seemed unaffected. He sat at his post in front of the science console, the blue light of the computer screen making his greenish-tinted skin an odd sort of gray.

Kirk couldn't stand the silence. He stood and walked to the science console, placing a hand on the back of Spock's chair. "Do we have any more information?"

"Very little, Captain," Spock said. He pushed a button and then swiveled his chair so that he faced Kirk. "Our long-range scans show that every planet in the system has been destroyed."

"Every planet?" Kirk asked. He couldn't make himself believe that much destruction had occurred in one system without the sun going nova.

"Fifteen major planets," Spock said, folding his hands together. "We will not know how many minor ones were destroyed until we are closer."

"How? How could fifteen planets disappear so quickly?" Kirk asked.

"They did not 'disappear,'" Spock said. "Sensors show large debris fields in the areas of each planet, slowly expanding to form rings. Intense waves of subspace interference are surging out of the system. The closer we get, the more intense the disturbance."

"Could this interference destroy planets, Mister Spock?"

"I do not know if the interference is the result of the destruction or the cause," Spock said. "When we arrive at the system I may be able to get more accurate readings."

"Spock?" he said softly, not really sure he wanted to know the answer to this question. "How many humanoids inhabited this system?"

"From the last survey results," Spock said, "I would estimate there to have been two billion, six hundred million spread out over the four inhabitable planets of the system."

"Two billion?" Probably all dead. Kirk couldn't let himself think about all those lives. He couldn't.

He moved over beside his command chair and stood facing the front screen, which showed the stars streaking past. Two hours until the *Enterprise* arrived. Two hours of waiting and wondering what had become of the billions of humanoids who lived in the Tautee system.

If all fifteen planets were destroyed, he knew what had happened to those people.

He dropped into the captain's chair and winced at the thinness of the padding against his back.

This would be a long two hours.

Dr. Leonard McCoy strode down the corridor toward cargo bay five. He was hardly ever on this deck, and the on-duty personnel were watching him as if they had never seen a medical officer before. They skittered out of his way, avoiding eye contact, and hurried to their posts. Ensigns, most of them, newly assigned, probably, with drudge duty that he didn't even want to think about doing.

They probably had been looking forward to the maintenance stop as much as he had.

No stopover on Starbase 11. He hated the thought of that. He had some experiments growing in his lab that needed the considered opinion of Dr. Beth Jones, one of the most brilliant scientific minds he had ever come across. Dr. Jones was on Starbase 11.

And McCoy wasn't.

Nor was he likely to be for some time. Even when this new mission, whatever the hell it was,

was over, the ship would probably dry-dock at some other starbase.

Dr. Jones had expressed interest in his research, and she had also mentioned an interesting test that could be done with a medical tricorder. A *modified* medical tricorder. But McCoy was a doctor, not an engineer, and he didn't even know how to take the damn things apart, let alone how to operate on them to change their function and readings.

So he contacted a real engineer, only to discover from the computer that Chief Engineer Montgomery Scott was in a cargo bay—and had been in the cargo bay since some time that night. He had left orders that he was not to be interrupted unless there was an emergency.

McCoy hesitated only a second before entering the cargo bay. Scotty obviously wasn't working on anything ship-related. If he had been, the order not to interrupt would have come from the captain. Which made, in McCoy's mind, the emergency qualification invalid. Especially to him.

The cargo-bay door slid open with a pneumatic hiss.

"I said I didna want to be disturbed." Scotty's voice sounded oddly dampened, as if it should echo but didn't.

For a moment, McCoy was too stunned to reply. In front of him were two of the biggest, ugliest machines he had ever seen. And between them was a large monitor, on which blue sky stretched for what seemed like miles over carefully trimmed green grass.

"What in Hanna's world . . . ?" McCoy said,

stopping just inside the door as it hissed closed. The two machines seemed to take up a large percentage of the cargo bay. Mister Scott was on his hands and knees, his head halfway inside one of the machines, making some sort of adjustments. McCoy could hear him talking to the machine.

After a moment the chief engineer pulled his head out, put his hands on his hips, and glared at McCoy. "Well, Doctor, now that you've seen it, do you like it?"

McCoy didn't really know what to make of it. He had no idea what it was. Or what it was for.

"I take that as a yes," Scotty said.

All McCoy could do was nod and stare into the big screen at the blue sky and green grass. He really needed a vacation. He knew that now. And from the looks of it, so did Scotty.

Scotty stood and brushed off his pants, then moved over beside McCoy. He stopped, hands on hips, smiling at the scene on the monitor as if it was a newborn babe.

"What is it?" McCoy finally managed to say.

"Why, it's a golf course," Scott said. His voice sounded almost sad that McCoy hadn't recognized what he was working on. "What else would it be?"

"A golf course?" McCoy asked. "What's the point?"

"Escape, lad," Scotty said. "Here, try this on." He handed McCoy the large helmet with the wires hooked to the large machines.

"I don't think—"

"Do it," Scotty said. "It won't hurt you."

Doubting his own sanity, McCoy stared at the rubber padded helmet for a moment, then slipped it over his head. The glasses came down over his face and suddenly, instead of staring at the green grass and blue sky through a monitor, he almost felt as if he were there. And for a moment he thought he could hear the wind blowing over the open fields.

Almost reluctantly, he pulled off the helmet and handed it to Scotty. "What is it?"

"Holographic projectors working in tandem," Scotty said, beaming, and pointing at the two machines. "I think I have them finally tuned. Now, if they'd just stay that way."

McCoy snorted in disgust. "Holograms. The future, they call it."

"That they are, lad. Maybe someday you won't need the helmet."

"Humph," McCoy said in response. "They keep saying holograms will be doing everything we do. As if they could replace *me* with one."

Scotty laughed and patted the doctor on the shoulder. "Doctor, no one could replace the likes of you."

The illusion of grass on the large monitor started to shimmer slightly and Scotty quickly ducked to the machine on the right, muttering to himself as he went.

After a moment, the picture stopped shimmering. Scotty slid out of the machine, grinning, a long dark streak running from his right eye to his chin. "Now, what's so important it couldn't wait until I finished the eighteenth green?"

"Eighteen? You did eighteen scenes like that?" McCoy pointed at the monitor.

"Aye," Scotty said. "Including the fairways and teeing areas. A golf course needs eighteen holes, ya know."

McCoy shook his head, then glanced down at the tricorder in his hand. Suddenly his lack of engineering skills seemed painfully obvious. Scotty could create something out of nothing. McCoy needed help modifying his tricorder.

"Mister Scott, since we're not going to Star Base Eleven, I—"

He didn't get the rest of his sentence out of his mouth. Suddenly the light in the room dimmed and then came back up. The grass and blue sky both suddenly looked as if they were a lake surface being blown by a stiff wind; then the picture went out. McCoy could smell the distinct odor of overheating equipment.

Scotty dove for the machine on the right but was too late. Something exploded and sparks flew everywhere.

"Mister Scott," the captain's voice came over the intercom. "We have a power drain."

"Aye," The word held a mixture of sadness, regret, and loss. Scott took a step back from the smoking machines. He shook his head.

"Mister Scott?" The captain's voice did not sound happy and McCoy smiled.

"Give me five minutes," Scott said, "and I'll fix your power drain."

"Then I'd like a report," the captain said. "Kirk out."

The smoke was thick and smelled of electrical cables. McCoy suppressed both a cough and his smile. He held out the tricorder.

"Is it broken?" Scott asked.

McCoy shook his head. "I need some modifications."

"Ach, so do these poor beasties. I'll clean up this mess and then come to sickbay."

McCoy slung the tricorder over his shoulder. "Thanks." He opened the bay door, thankful for the fresh air of the corridor. He coughed once, then stopped outside the door. "One more thing, Mister Scott."

"Aye, sir?"

"Why are you building a golf course?"

Scotty rose to his full height, as he often did when his pride was assaulted. "I am a Scotsman, lad. We invented the game."

McCoy nodded.

And then waited until he was in the turbolift before he started laughing.

Chapter Three

PRESCOTT SAT in her chair in the dimly lit amphitheater. The screens had been dead for hours now. The environmental controls were running on emergency power, and the gravity had gone from normal to low.

The chair was bolted into the floor for just this sort of emergency, and she wore the restraining bands on her ankles and thighs, roping her in place. The idea had been to bolt everything down in case the gravity controls failed. That way the researchers could continue their work even under the lowgrav conditions of the moon. She doubted that the designers ever thought the bands would come in handy in the almost zero gravity of the remaining hunk of the moon.

The center's planners had thought that the gravity controls would break down monthly. Instead, this was the first time anyone had had to use the system. Yet another miscalculation in a whole, disastrous series of them.

The room shook slightly, stirring the dust. Every few minutes the base rattled. It was already unstable. With each shake, she assumed the containment would break, and the cold darkness of space would rush in and take them all to a very quick but very painful death.

She licked her lips. They were dry and caked with grit. Dust, dirt, and debris floated around her, unhampered by bolts.

A computer had broken through one of the screens and was at the moment floating near the ceiling, sent there by that last moonquake. In a few minutes it would settle slowly back to the floor somewhere.

She had thought she was going to die in this room, but so far it hadn't worked out that way. Somehow, by some miracle, the base had held together when the moon broke apart.

All the ripping and tearing and screaming and shaking she had expected to hear, but couldn't, as she watched the fifteen planets in the Tautee system silently blow apart had happened when the moon shattered. But, apparently, a large chunk of the moon had held together.

Within that large chunk resided the center.

Lucky her. Lucky all of them. They had a few extra days to think about dying.

Folle was pleased; he somehow thought they

might survive. He was scavenging, seeing how bad the damage was in the rest of the center.

And who else was alive.

She estimated that a few hundred had lived. The computer terminal in front of her had shown her a schematic of the center just before a power surge shut the machine down. Several sections appeared to have collapsed. But several had survived.

A few hundred tired, injured, homeless Tauteeans to carry on until their air ran out, or their containment cracked and let in the cold of deep space.

For days after her home planet broke apart, killing over a billion, she didn't much care if she lived or died. All she kept seeing was the blue-green meadow surrounding her parents' home, the stream with the silver fish, and her old pet Sandpine. They were now all gone, destroyed by something she had headed. Destroyed by her "project."

"I don't know that for sure," she said aloud. Folle had said that to her fifty times as he tried to help her regain some strength. *We don't know for sure,* he had said. *We can't know.*

He had meant that they couldn't know because the equipment couldn't tell them. But she knew the real truth behind Folle's statement.

They couldn't know because not knowing kept them sane.

If she knew for certain that the Kanst Energy Experiment was responsible for the breakup of the Tautee system, she'd never be able to take another breath. She and her fellow workers would be the greatest mass murderers of all time. She would have killed all her people.

Her mind couldn't embrace that idea.

Refused it outright.

Even though she knew that everyone was dead, she could still see her parents' faces when she closed her eyes. It seemed no different from living the rest of her days in this destroyed facility, far from home.

Except that her heart ached. Literally ached, as if someone had stabbed her there.

She took a deep breath and glanced around at the empty room and the debris just now settling back toward the floor in the weak gravity.

Folle had been gone a long time. He had tried to take her out of this room, this place where she watched her entire race die, but she had refused to leave. For the past two days, he had brought her food and news of the two hundred people in the nearby command center.

He had told her of the blocked corridors and twisting steel beams. He had said that the others had hope of survival. And he had asked why she hadn't.

He knew the answer. He was as good a scientist as she was. The bit of moon that held them together wouldn't remain in one piece forever. If it didn't shake itself apart, it would hit other space debris and shatter.

There were a thousand other possibilities. Every scenario she ran ended with their deaths.

The main door clanged. She took a deep breath

of the dusty air, trying to brace herself for Folle's energy. He was trying to keep her alive. He was trying to keep all of them alive, for what she didn't know.

They had no right to live.

Even if they hadn't caused the destruction. Everyone else was dead. They had no right to survive.

She turned to watch him. He was still a beautiful man, thinner than he had ever been, but beautiful. He jumped off the top step, and half-floated toward her.

He grabbed her shoulder to stop his momentum, then held the chair as he braced himself against the desk beside her.

"I have a crew patching leaks in the A Section," he said.

She shrugged. "Busy work. We both know it won't last long."

"Long enough to be rescued," he said.

He had never said that word before. She bit back a sarcastic comment—*How could anyone save you? We killed everyone in the universe*—and instead asked, as reasonably as she could, "Do you really believe that some of the big ships from Tautee orbital labs survived?"

He nodded, glancing around at the empty, blank screens and the destroyed control panels. "We just need to let them know we're still down here."

Maybe if she talked to him, she could get him to abandon this new delusion. She stared at the hole in the screen before her, the one made by the floating computer. But what was the point of destroying his illusions now? So that he could die as miserably as she would?

"Prescott?" he asked softly.

She turned her gaze to him, smiled at him, and ran her knuckles along the soft skin of his face. One of them deserved to hope. If he kept busy, then maybe he wouldn't be frightened when the end came.

"Are any of the shafts to the surface still open?" she asked.

"No," he said, as if it didn't bother him. "They're all blocked. But we might be able to clear one. Twenty-zee-one seems to be blocked in only four places."

She shook her head sadly and turned to the blank screens. The moon base had never been designed to withstand the moon breaking up. Who could have foreseen such an event? It was a marvel that they were even still alive.

She punched a few dead buttons that before would have let her see the incoming ships. Sometimes it frustrated her more that everything was broken, that nothing worked. It seemed like such a metaphor for the experiment itself.

"You know, Folle," she said, "I just wish I could get one more glimpse of the stars."

"You want me to send a crew here to try to get a camera up and running?"

She shook her head. It would just be more busy work. She knew that seeing the surface wasn't going to be possible. The moon's breakup must have destroyed all the cameras on the surface. And severed the connections between here and there.

No, the only chance she had of getting out of this grave was to put on a surface suit and somehow dig her way through a kilometer of collapsed tunnels to what remained of the surface. And at the moment she just didn't have that much energy.

"You don't think we'll be able to repair that tunnel, do you?" he asked.

"I think this section of moon is staying together with spit, string, and a massive amount of luck," she said. "And I'm afraid that if we mess with it, we'll make matters worse."

He frowned, caught a chunk of floating steel, and shoved it in his pocket. His pockets were bulging. He must have been doing that everywhere he went. She wondered what he did with the steel when his pockets were full.

"Can we at least try rigging up an emergency signal?" he asked.

She swung her chair around and looked him in the eye, being careful in the light gravity not to move too fast. He needed her permission. He was acting as if they still had a mission, as if she were still in charge of something important.

She signed. "Go ahead if it'll make you happy. Gather up a crew and I'll come to the communications room to check on the progress."

Folle grinned, the dirt on his face showing lines she had never seen before. "Thanks. Give us an hour," he said. He turned and jumped carefully toward the entrance.

"Take your time," she said.

She turned back to face the blank screens. Sending an emergency signal was as useful as pressing the buttons on the control panel before her. She let her fingers dance over the dead buttons. Try as she might, she couldn't make the surface cameras work.

And no matter how strong the signal, Folle would be shouting into emptiness. Except for a few hundred people trapped in the remains of a moon, the universe was dead.

No one would rescue them, because no one was out there.

Chapter Four

AS PER SPOCK'S RECOMMENDATION, the *Enterprise* came out of warp farther away from the Tautee system than normal. Spock's point, which was extremely valid, was that if all fifteen planets had been destroyed, then there might be a great deal of debris, and the *Enterprise* didn't want to come out of warp in the center of it.

They had missed the main debris fields, but not by very much.

Kirk leaned forward in his chair, one booted foot pressed against the chair itself, the other braced beneath him. He had seen schematics of the Tautee system. It had looked like a thousand other systems—a yellow sun and fifteen major planets, three of which were gas giants.

The only remarkable thing was that four of the

inner planets were in the band of life and had atmospheres capable of sustaining life. Two of the planets were class-M planets, very similar to Earth. Usually a solar system had one or two such planets at the most, but this system was blessed with four.

The last report from ten years ago was that the Tautee system supported a humanoid population that had started on the fifth planet and spread through the system. The report stated that they were at least fifty to one hundred years from discovering warp drive and leaving their system.

In other words, there had been nothing remarkable about the Tauteeans. They were evolving just as hundreds of other young cultures were doing throughout the sector, slowly making their way up and out into the stars.

Until now.

"All stop," he said

Slowly he pushed himself out of his chair, his gaze never leaving the screen. This wasn't possible.

Out of the corner of his eye, he saw Sulu and Chekov staring as he did, mouths open.

He had only seen something like this once before. When the Planet Killer had swept through the galaxy, chomping planets. And even then, it hadn't left this kind of debris.

All fifteen major planets orbiting the Tautee sun had broken apart, leaving nothing more than chunks of floating rock and debris in ever-expanding rings. The screen couldn't begin to encompass all the damage.

The outer rings from the destruction of the larger, gas giants were already awe-inspiring, and horribly, horribly beautiful. If he had come upon this without knowing about the way the system had been, he would have stopped the ship and studied everything, just because the sight was so incredible.

But he did know what had been here before. An entire civilization had been here, spread across four of those planets. Billions of lives that were now vapor in the growing rings.

What had happened here?

What had gone wrong?

"Mister Spock," he said, his voice not at all steady. He turned toward his science officer, hoping that Spock's inscrutable Vulcan features showed a hint of what he was thinking. "Are there any survivors?"

But Spock had his head down, eyes pressed against the scanning device. Kirk understood. It was Spock's way of covering his own shock at the devastation.

"Mister Spock?"

"I am sorry, sir. I was double-checking my readings." Spock swiveled his chair and faced the captain. Although somber, Spock's expression was no different than it had been before they left warp. Maybe he wasn't covering anything at all.

"It would seem unlikely that there would be any survivors," Spock said. "Although the society had space travel, it was pre-warp. Ships that primitive could not survive this type of devastation."

"Billions of people, Spock. Could anyone have survived?"

Spock shook his head. "If they did not know this was coming, they would not have survived. The

Tauteeans lived mainly on the two class-M planets. When the planets broke apart, their atmospheres were scattered into space. People on the surface would no longer have air to breathe or sufficient gravity to hold them against that surface."

Kirk's fists clenched. Billions of lives lost.

Billions.

He had seen destruction before and knew that the numbers didn't tell half the story. Each of those lives had had loves and hates, goals and dreams, successes and failures. All rendered meaningless in the space of a few days.

What awful days they must have been.

There was a loud groaning sound, as if a billion ghosts had moaned at the same moment; then suddenly the *Enterprise* was rocked as if something huge had collided with it.

Kirk went sprawling to the right. He quickly tucked his shoulder and rolled with the fall.

Ensign York rolled past him and slammed into the wall.

Kirk rolled once more and then caught himself quickly. He came up on one knee, holding on to the engineering console. "What's happening?"

"I am uncertain, Captain," Spock shouted over the rumbling and moaning as he held on to his science console with one hand while punching in commands with the other.

Sulu had been knocked from his chair, but had quickly regained it. His fingers were flying over the board in front of him, trying to stabilize the ship.

Chekov had managed to stay in place and was studying his instruments while holding on.

The shaking and all the noise subsided and Kirk stood slowly, straightening his shirt and brushing off the dust on his arm. Ensign York shook himself and stood carefully. Uhura picked up her chair, tugged on her skirt, and sat down, replacing the receiver in her ear as she bent over her console.

"It seems," Mr. Spock said slowly, "that the *Enterprise* was hit by an intense subspace disturbance."

"The same kind as the ones we picked up before?" Kirk kept a hand on his chair as he made his way to the science console. Two-dimensional oscillations showed up on the science computer screen. They obviously meant something to Spock, but Kirk had not seen them before.

"The very same, sir," Spock said, "Only this is a thousand times more intense.

"Where's it coming from?" Kirk understood the oscillations on the screen now. They were a representation of the disturbance, moving like ocean waves in space in ever-expanding rings from the Tautee system.

Spock never took his eyes off the instruments in front of him. "I have yet to discover the origin of the disturbance." His voice had a troubled sound to it.

"Well, find it," Kirk said. He stepped back toward his chair, and tapped the comm button for engineering. "Mister Scott. Any damage?"

"Nothing to speak of, sir." Scotty's voice came back strong.

"Keep me posted. Kirk out." He looked up at the screen, at the damage floating in ever-widening rings where planets used to be. Whatever happened here was still happening. There was no doubt at all about that.

"Sir, I am picking up a very faint radio distress signal," Uhura said.

Radio? Ancient technology. "Pinpoint it, Lieutenant," Kirk said. He leaned against the arm of his chair. A distress signal. To what point? The survey team had said this was a pre-warp culture. Who was the distress signal meant for?

"Mister Spock, I thought you said there was no chance of survivors."

"On the contrary, Captain," Spock said, "I believe I said that it was unlikely there would be many survivors."

"Do you care to explain the distinction?"

"The term 'unlikely' means that there is a chance someone did survive. However, an entire series of circumstances would have had to occur. The chances of those circumstances happening at this opportune time would be—"

"Unlikely, yes, I know, Mister Spock." Kirk shook his head and turned back to Uhura. "Can you pinpoint the signal?"

"The distress signal is coming from a large asteroid in the debris of the fifth planet," Uhura said.

"Mister Spock, are you finding any signs of survivors in that area?"

"I find it impossible to determine at this distance, Captain. But the asteroid is large enough to sustain a significant number of people. I am quite certain we have survivors there."

"Quite certain, Mister Spock?" Kirk didn't want to hope without any reason. "And what is this certainty based on?"

"The fact that the distress signal just started." Spock quirked an eyebrow at him. Kirk got the uncanny feeling that Spock was making fun of him.

Kirk rounded his chair and was about to order Sulu to take the *Enterprise* to that asteroid when Spock added, "However, I do not believe we should approach the asteroid. The subspace disturbances that appear to have broken these planets apart may possibly be more intense in that region. With that much planetary debris, the ship would not survive."

Kirk glanced at Spock, who was again monitoring the oscillations on his screen. "What do you suggest, Mister Spock?"

"Holding on," Spock said. "We are about to be hit by another subspace wave."

Almost before Kirk could grab his captain's chair, the ship rocked and shuddered. As the lights flickered, he glanced around. This time, with Spock's warning, the bridge crew were staying at their stations.

As the wave passed and the lights came back up, McCoy's voice came over the intercom. "You want to tell me what in blazes is going on? I have patients bouncing all over down here."

Kirk punched the comm button. "We'll tell you just as soon as we know. For now, just hang on. Kirk out."

Mr. Chekov turned around. "Captain, we have company."

"On screen, Mister."

Kirk let go of the command chair and turned to face the main screen as the view of the destroyed planets disappeared and was replaced by four Klingon cruisers. They floated there as if they owned the space.

"Red alert," he ordered.

As if they didn't have enough problems already.

Chapter Five

CAPTAIN KELLY BOGLE stood in front of the main viewscreen on the *U.S.S. Farragut.* He had come out of warp at the edge of the Tautee system to find himself with two separate problems. The strange destruction of fifteen planets, and his sister ship, the *U.S.S. Enterprise,* surrounded by four Klingon cruisers.

Bogle knew that Kirk could handle the four Klingon ships—he'd seen Kirk handle bigger problems—but Bogle didn't like the implications. Four ships to one Federation vessel, a destroyed star system all around them.

That special Klingon weapon he'd heard about must have been a doozy.

He turned. His bridge crew was at their professional best, which meant they had been startled by the sudden turn of events just as he was.

His helmsman, Diego Rodriguez, watched their course as if they were flying through an asteroid belt.

The communications officer, Julie Gustavus, kept one hand to her ear as she monitored the intership communications.

Several ensigns read nearby computer screens with great focus, as if their entire careers depended on it.

While Kelly Bogle could match Jim Kirk drink for drink in any officer's lounge in the galaxy, while he could play poker with equal skill, and while he could tell tall tales as well as any officer in the fleet, he did one thing differently: he dominated his ship. Bogle didn't believe in the camaraderie that Kirk used to bind his people. Bogle did it with sheer determination, a quest for perfection, and rigid discipline.

And it had worked for years.

He would need all of that discipline right now.

Bogle sat back and studied the situation for a moment. His main focus had to be the *Enterprise*. The systemwide disaster had developed over the course of days and possibly weeks. The *Enterprise* had only been in the sector a few minutes before the *Farragut*.

That meant that the Klingons had been there first. They would have to deal with the Klingons first in return.

"Any sign of hostilities?" Bogle asked.

Commander Richard Lee glanced up from his science console. A shock of red hair fell over his forehead. Lee's haircut was always too long, and his uniform always needed just a little extra attention, all items he'd been cited for many times before. But Bogle didn't dare discipline him too hard. Lee was the best science officer that Bogle had ever worked with. The last thing he wanted to do was chase him away.

"No hostilities yet, sir," Lee said. "However, the *Enterprise* is at full alert." Lee glanced back down at his scope, then continued without looking back up. "So are the Klingons. I'd say something is going to happen any minute now."

Bogle nodded and turned to Rodriguez. "Move us into position right behind the *Enterprise.* Let's let the Klingons know we're here."

"Aye, sir," he said.

The rest of the crew continued their monitoring.

Bogle sat in the captain's chair, extending his long legs outward. Within a few moments, the *Enterprise* filled the screen with the four Klingon vessels beyond and above it.

"Nice work, Ensign," Bogle said.

"We're being hailed by the *Enterprise,*" Gustavus said.

"On screen," Bogle said, leaning back.

Captain Kirk's face filled the screen. He looked pale, and his hair was ruffled, as if he'd been running his hands through it. Not at all the smiling, relaxed Jim Kirk that Bogle was used to.

Was it the Klingons?

Or the system destruction itself? Bogle really

hadn't had time to absorb the system's destruction or its meaning yet. He suspected he would have to do that in private.

Then Kirk grinned, and Bogle saw the friend he had spent many a satisfying shore leave with. "Kelly, nice to have you with us."

"Good to be here, Jim," Bogle said. He'd worked with Jim Kirk a number of times in the past and it had always been successful despite their different command methods. Kirk seemed to have an ability to come out on top. As far as Bogle was concerned, that was a great trait for a teammate to have.

Someone spoke behind Kirk and his grin faded. "Tell your crew to hang on to something." His voice was serious and very cold. *"Now."*

Bogle didn't hesitate or even ask why. He grabbed the arms of his own captain's chair, and then punched his intercom. "This is the captain. Find yourself something solid and hang on to it. We—"

The ship moaned and then jolted backward.

Bogle's finger flew off the button, effectively ending the communications.

The ship rattled and moaned like a sick teenager, first to one side and then the other. His officers twisted and leaned, but didn't lose their places.

He had only felt something like this once before—in a battle with the Bnez when he was an ensign. The Bnez had rammed his ship.

Sparks flew from Commander Lee's panel, but he just fanned the smoke away and continued working.

Another hard jolt sent an ensign sprawling.

"Intense subspace wave, sir," Lee shouted over the rumbling and moaning. "It should be passing right about . . . now."

As Lee spoke, the shaking diminished and stopped. Silence descended over the bridge like a heavy blanket.

Bogle tapped his comm button and hailed his chief engineer, Projeff Ellis. Ellis could lead a team of engineers through a desert and come out the other side with a pool full of water and a blonde swimming in it. "Pro, what's the damage?"

"None, sir." The chief's voice came back strong. "Just a few bruises and some wounded pride."

"Thanks," Bogle said. He turned to Gustavus. She still clutched her console, her knuckles white with the strain. "Hail the *Enterprise* for me."

"There's no need, sir," she said. "They're still on-screen."

Kirk's hair looked even more tousled, and his cheeks were red, as if he'd been exerting himself. Bogle suspected he didn't look much better.

"That was some welcome," Bogle said.

"Thanks," Kirk said, smiling. "Expect it every five-point-four minutes. This is a charming section of space."

"I'm gathering that," Bogle said. He glanced at Lee, who nodded. Apparently his science officer's assessment of the sector was the same as Kirk's.

Behind Kirk, Bogle heard a woman say, "Captain, we are being hailed by the Klingons."

Kirk nodded to Bogle. "I'll patch this through to you. It should be interesting."

Bogle laughed. "Thanks." The screen went blank.

Everything with Kirk was always interesting. Never by the book, but always interesting.

Chapter Six

"PUT THE KLINGONS on screen," Kirk said after Captain Bogle's face disappeared. "And patch this through to the *Farragut*."

"Aye, sir," Uhura said.

Kirk rose so that he would face the Klingons head-on. He spread his feet slightly, his hands on his hips. He would let Bogle, an old friend, see the shock Kirk felt at the destruction of the entire section, but he would let the Klingons only see his anger.

His very deep anger.

But he did have to handle this well. There were possible survivors to think of.

The rescue would be delicate at best.

Impossible at worst.

After a moment, Klingon Supreme Commander

KerDaq appeared on the screen. He wore the standard Klingon military uniform, with two insignias near his right shoulder Kirk had never seen before. The lines and ridges in KerDaq's face were more pronounced than those of most Klingons Kirk had met. He and KerDaq had crossed each other's path only once before, without problems, at a Federation/Klingon conference. For a Klingon, KerDaq was reasonable. If he belonged to any other species, he would be considered truculent.

Unfortunately, KerDaq was as good as Klingons got.

"Captain Kirk," KerDaq said, his speech slow and slightly accented. It was also tinged with sarcasm. "I should have known you'd be involved with this."

"A pleasure, as always, Commander," Kirk said, not letting himself be baited. He knew Klingons. They always came on strong and didn't respect weakness of any kind.

"Save your pleasantries," KerDaq said. "I do not discuss small things with people who would destroy an entire star system."

For a moment Kirk didn't totally register what KerDaq had just said. Then it sunk in. KerDaq was blaming the Federation for this destruction. Kirk couldn't let that stand.

"If you believe that the Federation had something to do with the destruction of this system," Kirk said, "you are wrong. Check your own records. We just arrived."

"A ploy," KerDaq said.

"Is it?" Kirk asked. "Or is this all a ploy on your

part to cover your use of that secret weapon we've heard so much about?"

KerDaq looked stunned for a moment; then his face colored. Before he could say anything, Mr. Spock said, "Another wave, Captain. Five seconds."

"I would suggest," Kirk said to KerDaq, "that you hang on to something solid."

The subspace wave struck the *Enterprise* as Kirk sat down in his command chair and held on. The thin padding bounced against his already bruised back. He'd been on an old roller coaster back near San Francisco on Earth. This felt a lot like it, only with grinding and tearing sounds. For just a moment the lights dimmed, then they came back up strong.

"Hold it together, Scotty," Kirk said too softly for anyone to hear.

On the screen Kirk saw KerDaq stumble as the wave hit, then grab on to one of the huge support pillars running through the Klingon bridge. He held on there, sneering at Kirk until the wave had passed, then let go.

"Kirk," he said, moving a step closer to the camera so that his face filled the screen. "If you and your Federation destroyed this system, you will pay. I will be watching."

With that the screen went blank.

Kirk tilted his head slightly, a bit bemused that he had ever thought KerDaq reasonable. Then he turned to Spock. "I don't think that went very well."

"Obviously," Spock said.

"The Klingons have moved a short distance away," Chekov said. "They are holding positions."

The screen once again showed the destruction throughout the Tautee system. The rings were expanding slowly, the rocks and asteroids spreading in an ever-lengthening band that would eventually encircle the sun.

Kirk clenched a fist. It was time to get on with what they were here for. The Klingons could watch all they wanted, as long as they stayed out of the way.

"Mister Spock," Kirk said. "I need to know what's causing those subspace waves. And I need a way to rescue those survivors."

Mr. Spock glanced at him. "That will take some time, sir."

"We don't have time, Mister Spock." Kirk glanced at the destruction spread out in front of him. "And I doubt those survivors do either."

Chapter Seven

Folle didn't come back.

Prescott released the restraints on her chair, but kept a grip on one arm. She had sat in the semi-darkness for hours waiting for him. She had expected him to return, telling her that the signal wouldn't work, or that the attempt was in vain.

Instead, he was gone.

On a deep level, one she didn't want to examine, she was afraid that something had happened to him. Strange that the thought of his death disturbed her so personally. He would be one more body, one more corpse on her head.

Nothing more.

But he was Folle, and he was still alive when the moon shattered, and he had supported her.

She hadn't supported him.

She had ridiculed his attempts to survive. What had her biology instructor in early children's class said? *The basic instinct of all creatures is survival.*

Even for her.

She let go of the chair arm. The extremely low gravity felt odd. Moving was like swimming, only without the weight of the water around her. The air supported her—or at least that was what it felt like—as she pushed off from her chair, buoyed her up when she jumped, and almost made her feel as if she could fly.

It took her no time at all to reach the doors to the amphitheater.

Then she stopped. She hadn't been outside this room since the moon shattered. Folle had been her window into the rest of the center. She had hidden from her colleagues and staff like a child expecting discipline from a parent.

Time to face the world again.

Or what was left of it.

She took a deep breath of the dry, stale air and pulled open the big door.

The dim lights made the corridor seem narrower than she remembered. Some chunks of steel had fallen out of the ceiling. Long cracks ran alongside the walls. Dust and debris floated here, too, like they did inside, only here they bounced off the walls, and had odd trajectories. The air seemed thicker, harder to breathe. The low ceiling now felt like a threat instead of a comfort.

At any minute, it might topple on her.

But she faced that same threat inside the amphitheater.

It was time for her to move. Time for her to go to Folle.

If he still lived.

She took another deep breath of the dust-caked air. Her throat was dry. Folle had brought her food and water the last two days. She had done nothing to survive. And now he wasn't thinking of her at all.

She would go to the communications center. If he wasn't there, working on the signal—well, she would worry about that then.

At first, as she made her way down the corridor, she tried to pretend to walk. But that was like walking in neck-deep water. Her body wanted to float. It was hard to stay on the ground. The designers had built railings for the times when the gravity ran out, but most of the railings had been dislodged in the destruction.

Finally, she gave in, jumped forward, and kept one hand above her so that she didn't rise too high and hit her head on the ceiling.

The trip went quickly.

Most of the doors were closed or off their hinges, the emergency lighting obscured by clouds of dust that followed her. She was starting to understand why Folle had been picking small metal objects out of the air and putting them in his pockets. She had dodged more than one piece of metal. Another slammed her in the head. She hadn't been traveling very fast and the piece of metal had been coming at her at an even slower speed, but the combination of her speed and the metal's speed caused a collision that left a cut on her scalp.

A few small droplets of blood floated away as she quickly ripped a small piece of cloth off her pants leg and held it against the wound. It didn't really hurt. It was just annoying, because it functioned as a reminder that she was still alive when so many others weren't.

She was almost to the communications room when the station started vibrating. The railing beside her banged against the wall, sending a clanging through the narrow passage. More debris floated by, this time at quicker speeds. She wedged herself into a corner, hoping that nothing would fall on her, nothing would hit her.

Then the vibrating stopped.

As it always did.

She knew some time soon it wouldn't stop.

She clung to the steel walls for a moment, shaken, her eyes so dry that they hurt. She felt different from the way she had before, and she wasn't sure why.

Until she realized.

She had protected herself.

For the first time since she watched the first planet shatter, she had taken care of herself. Instead of acquiescing to her death, she had actually tried to prevent it.

She wasn't sure if that was a good sign or not.

She pushed a loose strand of hair off her face, and wiped the dust from her nose. Her skin was caked in dirt. Her hair was probably silver with debris. Her clothing was in shreds.

And there was nothing she could do to change any of it.

She continued to make her way toward the communications room. The corridor widened near it. The door was open, and the light from inside seemed brighter.

Maybe that was because she knew there were people inside.

She used the door to lever herself inside.

Three of her officers crowded around one lone console panel. The other consoles were on their sides, shattered, or ripped open for parts. Some of the bolted chairs remained in place. Others were shoved against the consoles, braced so that they wouldn't float free in the low gravity.

Folle had his thin frame in the only chair in front of the console, and beside him Carad and Rogaur floated, watching. Both still wore their white lab coats, now stained with dust and black streaks. Carad's bald head had a nasty cut across the top that made her remember her own. She again tapped it with the scrap of cloth. It seemed the wound was clotting or filling with dust. For the moment either would work.

The communications panel in front of the three men was the only panel in the room showing any power. Folle was typing something on the panel.

"Did you have some luck?" she asked, floating up to the back of Folle's chair and pulling herself down into a standing position.

Folle started as if he had heard a ghost. He glanced over his shoulder at her. And then he smiled, the look full of warmth and welcome.

"We think we're sending on ten different bands," he said, as if her presence was not unusual, "but we have no way of knowing for sure. But we have to constantly keep inputting the data to keep it running."

"How long did it take you to get the signal running?"

"A while," Folle said. "I'm sorry I forgot to bring you supplies. I lost track of the time."

"That's fine," she said. Carad glanced at her as if surprised that Folle had been taking care of her. "I'm out now. I'll manage just fine."

"I knew you would," Folle said. He had returned his attention to the console. Somehow, it had become more important than she was. She wondered when that had happened.

"You really think this will work?" she asked, hearing and wincing at the hope in her own voice.

"In order for people to find us, they have to know we're here."

What people? she wanted to ask, but she didn't. They were busy. They weren't brooding. They would spend their last few days well, instead of feeling sorry for themselves like she was.

Like she was.

Oh, hell. It was time she started taking care of herself as well. Death wasn't coming as quickly or as easily as she would like. It was her philosophy professor at the Studies Center who had said it was better for a person to live in perfect understanding of his crime than to die for that crime in complete ignorance.

She finally understood what the professor had meant.

He had meant there were times when living was a greater torture than dying.

It was time to accept her fate.

"I'm going back to the observation room. Maybe I can get something working there. If there's someone out there, maybe I'll find them." She let go of Folle's chair. "Keep me posted."

The men knew she had no chance of getting any of the observation equipment running again, just as she knew their signal had no hope. But like her they didn't say anything.

"Good luck," Folle said without turning away from his work.

"You too." She pushed off slowly for the door. Better to keep busy than to brood. The only difference was Folle had himself convinced that some mythical rescuer would appear.

She knew rescue was impossible.

The only people left alive in the entire universe were in this station, as trapped as she was.

And when the center broke open, as it inevitably would, they would all die.

Together.

Chapter Eight

CAPTAIN BOGLE remained in his captain's chair, fingers gripping the arms. These subspace waves disturbed him, in more ways than one. If they could destroy a planet, they could destroy a ship. And he didn't like putting his ship and crew in unnecessary danger at any time.

He was having his officers monitor the waves to see if they were growing in intensity. And also to discover any other information they could about them.

Kirk's interaction with the Klingons bothered him too. Something about the interchange hadn't seemed right. Kirk had done fine considering the Klingon's hostility, but it seemed as if Kirk's ego had gotten in the way.

"The *Enterprise* is hailing us, sir," Ensign Gustavus said.

"Put it on screen," Bogle said.

He stood as Kirk's face filled the screen. Kirk looked just as tousled as he had the last time they'd talked. Bogle imagined he didn't look much better since they'd ridden out three of the subspace waves now.

"Nice job with the Klingons," Bogle said, not smiling.

Kirk smiled and half laughed. "They always love my charm." Then Kirk's smile faded. "My science officer and chief engineer have a way to get us inside the system. To where that signal is coming from."

"Do they have a way back out?" Bogle said.

"We'll get out." Kirk sounded impatient. He clearly had a plan and wanted to tell Bogle about it.

Bogle motioned for his science officer, Lee, to join him. "You think we should respond to that emergency signal we've been picking up?"

"The signal started after we appeared," Kirk said.

"It could have been triggered by one of those waves," Bogle said.

"It could have," Kirk said. "Or survivors might have triggered the signal themselves. We don't know. But we need to find out."

Bogle glanced at Lee. Lee was frowning. Rodriguez was monitoring the Klingon ships on his navigational computer. Klingons, subspace waves, and an emergency beacon. Kirk was well known for his tendency to rush in, to solve the problem no matter how difficult. Bogle had gotten his command by being more cautious. And this seemed like a very logical time to be very, very cautious.

"Maybe we should see if we can verify the distress signal. It might be a Klingon trap of some sort."

Kirk waved his hand in the air as if brushing aside Bogle's worries. "My science officer tells me that asteroid could shatter in any of these waves. If there are survivors, they'll be killed. The faster we move the better."

"He's right, Captain," Lee said softly. "If there are survivors, we have to get them out. Quickly."

Bogle glanced sharply at Lee and then turned back to Kirk. He didn't like the idea of risking his ship in those waves. He would rather face Klingons than lose the *Farragut* to some unknown weapons system.

He sighed. Kirk arrived first.

Kirk had already assessed the situation.

Kirk had a phenomenal success rate.

And Kirk was right this time.

The survivors, if there were any, might be the last of their destroyed race.

"All right," Bogle said, doing his best to keep the irritation out of his voice. "What's your plan?"

As he asked the question, he wondered if they should have been scrambling the message. The Klingons were probably listening. But, then, what harm would that do? All they would learn would be about the rescue mission.

"We try the old two-steps-forward-one-back routine," Kirk said.

Bogle felt like that maneuver had been left out of his playbook. Was Kirk using a code after all? He knew Starfleet procedure for letting another commander know that the message was going to be encoded. This wasn't it.

"Run that by me again."

Lee cleared his throat beside Bogle and then, without waiting for permission to speak, said, "I understand it, sir. We go in between waves and then to reduce the effect of the wave we ride it outward for a short distance. Surfing the wave. It's brilliant. And I think it might work."

"Exactly," Kirk said. "The waves might be more intense the closer we get into the system, and so we'll be in them longer, riding with them, but it should work just long enough to see if there are survivors."

"I'm still lost here," Bogle said. Now he made no pretense in hiding his irritation. "Explain this scheme to me one more time."

Lee broke in before Kirk could say anything. He'd have to talk to Lee about this later.

"Imagine," Lee said, "that you are standing in shallow water on the beach and a five-foot wave is coming at you. If you stand there it will probably knock you down. However, if you turn and float with it, surf with it toward the shore, you won't feel its force as much."

"And a starship will hold together through all this?" Bogle asked Kirk, not looking at his first officer. The *Farragut* had gone through a number of difficult, stressful maneuvers, but nothing quite like the one Lee described.

Kirk laughed, but there was no real joy in his voice. "My chief engineer, Mister Scott, assures me she will and so far he's never let me down."

Bogle wished he had time to check with his own engineer, Projeff, while this conversation was happening. And he would, before the ship went anywhere near those debris fields.

Lee was leaning forward beside Bogle, caught up in the idea. "It would be better to go in over the plane of the system," Lee said, "and come down from on top of the debris field left by the destruction of the planets. Less chance of collision that way."

Kirk glanced off screen for a moment, then nodded. "We'll do that. But Kelly, you'll be out here alone with the Klingons."

"You don't think both ships should go in?" Bogle asked, trying to ignore the thread of relief running up his spine.

"No," Kirk said. "I think two ships might confuse the matter. And besides, no point in risking two ships at this point."

"I can handle the Klingons," Bogle said.

That much, anyway, was for the better, as far as he was concerned.

Kirk ran a hand through his hair. It only made the tousling worse. "I'll tell the Klingons what we're going to do, and I'll ask them to help in the rescue."

Whatever Bogle had expected Kirk to say next, it wasn't that. The joke around Starfleet command was that the word "help" wasn't even in the Klingon lexicon—at least when it came to non-Klingons who needed the help.

"Help?" Bogle asked. "Are you kidding?"

Kirk shrugged. "What could it hurt?"

Now Bogle knew that Kirk was completely crazy. He'd always half thought so, but now he knew. Shaking his head, he said, "I guess it won't hurt to ask. If they decide to join you, it'll keep them busy for a while."

"And if they don't, you'll be out here with four Klingon vessels."

Bogle snorted without meaning to. "Don't worry about us, Jim. We can hold our own just fine."

Kirk's grin was sudden and mischievous. "I know," he said. "I've played cards with you. Remember? Stand by. I'll link you into the conversation with the Klingons."

The screen went dead. Bogle sat in the captain's chair, still shaking his head.

The circular bridge of the Klingon cruiser was filled with activity. No one spoke. The green walls and the dim lights made the bridge seem wartime dark. That was probably appropriate. War was as close as the tip of an enemy's dagger.

KerDaq's second-in-command, and his closest ally on the ship, KobtaH, searched for the center of the rift. KerDaq could trust none of his other officers to find it and report the result to him in a timely fashion. Several of his bridge crew had recently arrived, and all needed to prove themselves before he trusted them. His commander's chair was too precious to lose to a zealous young Klingon with a name to make.

The other bridge officers were monitoring the situation as well. They all knew this was the kind of encounter that could go very badly for all of them, or extremely well.

KerDaq intended to make it go well.

But they had done nothing except talk to the Federation starships since they arrived. And they could do nothing else.

Yet.

They had to wait.

KerDaq hated waiting. He was a warrior, not someone who sat and waited. But he knew every warrior had to have patience, had to know when to fight and when not to fight.

This was not yet the time to fight.

The Federation ships first had to show him where their secret superweapon was hidden.

He had a plan.

The Federation would have to retrieve their weapon. KerDaq and his officers had studied the subspace waves. Their ship could go into the waves and survive if they moved with the waves as they passed. It would be risky, but it would be worthwhile.

Then, when the Federation ships had the weapon, he would take it from them.

KerDaq would have the Federation weapon. He

would personally take the weapon to the High Council. Then he would be a hero.

"Commander," KjaH, his science officer, said, his voice rumbling through the silence, "we are still unable to pinpoint the origin of the subspace waves."

KerDaq swung around in his high-backed command chair and glared at his science officer. "What can be so hard?"

"Sir, our position does not allow us a good reading. If we could move . . ."

"We will not move," KerDaq said. He spoke firmly. "Find the center, for at that center is the Federation superweapon."

"Yes, sir," KjaH said, snapping his heels smartly on the floor. He turned back to his panel.

KerDaq nodded and swung back to face the main screen, which showed the two Federation ships and the destroyed system beyond. He tugged at the edge of his gloves, making certain their steel points rested across his knuckles. His science officer knew when to back down and when to fight. That was the sign of a good warrior. He would have to keep a sharp eye on him.

"Sir," Communications Officer KenIqu said. "The *Enterprise* hails us."

"On screen," KerDaq said loudly. Then to himself he added, "Let us see what kind of treachery they are up to now."

Kirk's sneering face filled the screen.

KerDaq growled to himself. This Kirk was quickly becoming one of the most hated and feared officers in the Federation. KerDaq could see no reason for the fear at the moment. Kirk had no more strength than any other Federation weakling.

"Commander," Kirk said, nodding slightly.

At least, KerDaq thought, the man knows how to show respect.

"We're going into the debris fields in the system," Kirk said. "We think we may have found survivors there. We're going to attempt a rescue of them. And—" He paused for obvious dramatic effect. "—we could use your help."

Kirk's words so surprised KerDaq that he laughed, a full belly laugh as if a warrior had just told a humorous story over a strong drink.

Kirk's ugly human eyes narrowed. "What is so funny, KerDaq?" he asked.

KerDaq leaned forward so that Kirk could see his insignias, the badges of his house and his honor. This Kirk thought him an idiot, easily tricked. KerDaq would prove that wrong immediately.

"You cannot fool us with your rescue ploy. You are going in to retrieve your weapon."

This time it was Kirk's turn to look shocked. KerDaq knew he had caught him in a lie. Human captains hid their emotions, unsuccessfully, but valiantly. This wide-eyed shock, this obvious reaction, was part of the trick, inexpertly done.

Kirk shook his head. "I told you, KerDaq, we don't have a weapon. But we have received a distress call, and we will not ignore it. We're going in. We would like you to come with us."

"You have another ship," KerDaq said. "You do not need us."

"We don't know how many survivors there are," Kirk said. "The more ships we have, the more space we have to beam survivors aboard."

"You are quite inventive," KerDaq said. "But we have done our own scans of your waves. Any ship that ventures into that system would be destroyed. Unless, of course, it understood the weapon, and had a way to shield itself from the weapon's effect."

"We don't have any special shield," Kirk said. "But we do have a plan. If—"

"Enough, Kirk." KerDaq swept his arm in the general direction of the ruined system. "Do as you please. But we will be watching and waiting. Do not think you can leave this area with that weapon."

KerDaq pounded the button on his chair and cut Kirk's answer off. There was no use listening to any more lies. He would not let Kirk lead one single Klingon warrior to his death. He would watch where Kirk went, shielded, into the center of the destruction.

And he would watch Kirk remove his weapon.

He would let Kirk's actions prove his guilt.

"Commander," KenIqu said, "the *Enterprise* is moving."

KerDaq nodded. "Inform the *QuaQa* that we will be following the *Enterprise*. The other two ships are to remain close to the second Federation vessel."

"Yes, sir," KenIqu said.

"Subspace wave approaching," KobtaH said.

KerDaq sat back, smiling, holding on to his chair while he watched the *Enterprise* move slowly off.

Soon the great Captain Kirk would be caught and disgraced. And the weapon that could do this destruction would be where it belonged: in the hands of the Empire.

Chapter Nine

THE *ENTERPRISE* BROKE AWAY from the *Farragut* and flew above the plane of the solar system, staying a safe distance from the remains of the planets. The bridge crew's expressions were tight, focused. They knew there was a high risk in this rescue operation, especially since there might not be anyone left to rescue.

They were willing to take the chance. They trusted Kirk. They always had.

And he trusted them as well.

"Full shields," he said. "Keep her steady, Mr. Sulu."

"Aye, sir." Sulu's gaze was focused on the screen.

"Captain," Chekov said. "Two Klingon ships are following us." He glanced over his shoulder, his eyes wide with surprise and tension.

Kirk smiled. So, KerDaq had decided to tag along after all. He wouldn't come down into the debris fields, but he would stand watch. Well, as far as Kirk was concerned they could watch all they want. There was no superweapon, and he doubted the Federation would ever work on one.

"Captain?" Chekov's accent got thicker when he grew nervous.

"Monitor them, Ensign," Kirk said.

"But Captain—"

"Monitor them," Kirk said, his smile growing. KerDaq knew how to get through those waves as much as they did. Perhaps he was worried that in saving the survivors, Kirk would discover the Klingon's weapon. Always, Kirk had learned, always listen to your enemies' professed fears, because often they were talking about what they would do—or what they had done—themselves.

Chekov was sputtering. He bent over his console.

"Oh, and Ensign," Kirk said, enjoying Chekov's consternation a bit more than he should, "put the ship on yellow alert. Shields up and extra power to the forward shield. I want the crew to be prepared for anything."

"Aye, sir!" Chekov said with such relieved fervor that Kirk had to stifle a laugh.

"Entering the debris field of the remains of the fifth planet," Sulu said.

Kirk gripped the arms of his chair, even though the ship hit no bumps. "Keep her steady, Sulu," Kirk said.

Huge asteroids drifted past the screen. Between

the huge chunks of what was left of the fifth planet were millions of tiny rocks and dust. They bounced off the shields like stones skipping over water. Kirk wasn't bothered much by the small ones at this speed. The fear was running into one too large for the shields to deflect.

Sulu didn't answer. He was obviously concentrating on keeping the ship on a course through the large rocks.

"Dead ahead," Spock said.

"Full stop," Kirk said. The huge asteroid looked barren from this distance. Kirk couldn't believe life could have survived there.

"I believe we will need to move closer if we are going to attempt the rescue," Spock said.

Kirk hated it when Spock used the word "attempt." He was so precise that he meant each word he said. Words like "attempt" meant Spock had doubts as to whether or not the project would succeed.

Kirk pushed himself out of the captain's chair.

No sense hesitating.

Or dwelling on the word "attempt."

They would succeed or die trying.

"Mister Sulu," Kirk said. "Take us in as close as you can to that hunk of rock."

"Aye, sir." Sulu looked somber as he punched in the coordinates. He would manually maneuver the close-in work. It was too sensitive for the computers.

In times like this Kirk sometimes ached to pilot the ship himself. But Sulu was one of the best. Sulu would bring them in safely.

"Mister Sulu," Spock said, "we face our first subspace wave in the debris field. It shall arrive in one minute. I have fed a course into your computer. On my mark, follow that course at one-tenth impulse for exactly three seconds."

"Course laid in and waiting for your command, Mister Spock," Sulu said.

Kirk glanced at Spock, who had his face buried in his viewfinder. He had trusted his life to Spock more times than he could remember. This time he was trusting the entire ship to him. One slip and the subspace wave would shake them apart, or slam them into a huge piece of the planet.

"Captain," Uhura said, "the distress signal is coming from inside the asteroid."

"Magnify screen, Mister Chekov."

A gray, jagged-surfaced rock filled the screen, slowly rotating to the right.

"Fifteen seconds until my mark, Mister Sulu," Spock said.

Kirk turned to Uhura. "Can you get an exact fix on the location, Lieutenant?"

"It's too deep underground, sir." She swiveled toward him, her brow furrowed, almost as if she didn't believe the readings. "At least a kilometer deep."

Kirk punched his comm button to engineering. "Scotty," he said, "can you rig the transporters to work through a kilometer of rock?"

"I wouldn't want to beam in there," Scotty said, his voice sounding far away. "But if it's the survivors you'll be trying to beam out, we can do it. If I can get a fix on them, that is."

"Now, Mister Sulu!" Spock said.

The *Enterprise* surged forward, leaving the jagged hunk of rock behind.

Then the subspace wave hit.

Far worse than before.

The ship bumped and rocked like a boat on a stormy ocean. Kirk gripped his chair, but that didn't steady him. His body bumped in and out of the chair as if it were a malfunctioning ejection seat.

Sulu braced his feet against the console in front of him, but kept himself in place. Chekov bounced out of his chair. Spock tumbled backward, caught himself, but was unable to stand.

Giant hunks of the destroyed planet flashed past the screen, and the shield howled and grew red with the impacts of small rocks and dust.

Then the wave had passed.

Spock stood, dusted himself off, and returned to the science station as if nothing had happened. Chekov shook his head once as if he were clearing it, then climbed back into his chair.

"Mister Sulu," Kirk said, "get us back to that asteroid."

"Aye, sir."

The *Enterprise* wove her way through a maze of rocks. The light vibrating continued from the pounding of rocks against the shield.

"How are our friends the Klingons, Mister Chekov?"

"The fleas are still with us, sir. But they are staying safely above the debris field."

Kirk nodded. The *Enterprise* continued to wind her way through the debris cloud. The movement didn't take very long, but it felt like forever.

Finally the huge asteroid filled the screen again. The asteroid was vaguely triangular, with large chunks of rock hanging off its side like knives.

"Captain," Spock said, "we are now close enough that I have been able to get more precise readings from the asteroid. It was a part of the fifth planet's moon, and is now the largest remaining chunk of that moon. There is some sort of base a kilometer underground. Most of the base has been destroyed. But the signal does originate from there."

"Survivors, Spock?" Kirk asked. He could suddenly feel his heart pounding against his chest. So far they had been acting under supposition. Now they might be able to get confirmation.

"I have very faint readings, Captain," Spock said. "There seem to be ninety-two separate life signs, all clustered in the same general area."

"Send the information to the transporter room." Kirk punched the comm button so hard that he bent his index finger backward. "Scotty, there are people inside that asteroid. Get them out of there."

"Aye, sir!"

"Kirk to sickbay. McCoy, we have survivors beaming aboard. I would imagine many are injured."

McCoy's voice came back strong. "Understood."

"Mister Sulu," Spock said, "we shall encounter another wave in one minute and forty-six seconds. I have sent new coordinates to your screen. On my mark, follow that course at one-ninth impulse."

"Course laid in, Mister Spock."

"Come on, Scotty," Kirk said to himself. He'd rather not ride another subspace wave through this debris field.

"Captain," Spock said, keeping his face buried in the viewfinder. His voice rose with fascination. "Owing to our new location, I have finally located the source of the subspace waves. They originate from what appears to be a rift in space in the area where the ninth planet used to be."

"A rift?" Kirk asked. The Klingons had a weapon strong enough to create a rift in space?

How was that possible?

Kirk punched the comm button. "Scotty. How's it going?"

"One minute, Mister Sulu," Spock said.

"We're getting them, sir," Scotty's voice replied.

Kirk sat staring at the huge chunk of a moon filling the screen. Hard to believe it had saved ninety lives by staying together. Sometimes the universe did strange things.

Spock held up his hand. "Five seconds, Mister Sulu."

"Scotty!" Kirk barked into the comm. "Are you finished?"

"No, sir. Beaming ninety-two people through a kilometer of rock is precision work. If I—"

"Then we'll come back for the rest," Kirk said.

"Now, Mister Sulu." Spock's arm went down as he spoke as if were starting a race.

And again the *Enterprise* flashed away from the asteroid, riding the crest of the subspace wave like a surfer headed for the beach.

A very rocky beach that Kirk hoped they'd never hit.

Chapter Ten

THE TINY NOISES she made seemed overwhelming in the cavernous room.

Prescott had crawled underneath the main-screen control panel. She had portable lights attached to her wrists—she couldn't find any helmet lamps—and she had been working for some time. She had discovered that Folle's philosophy was right; it was better to be busy. That way, she didn't have time to dwell on the hopelessness of their situation.

Or on its cause.

When she had crawled under the panel, she had been surprised. Despite the shaking and dust, the panel appeared to be in fine shape. The problem was with the lack of power (how ironic), the shattered connections to the surface, and the aboveground cameras, as she had expected. Still, she double-checked every circuit, every system, and every chip.

"Any success?" Folle's voice rang to her from above. She hadn't even heard him enter. That pleased her. She had been concentrating hard.

She shut off her wrist lights, pushed herself free of the access panel, and half-floated into an upright position. Her hands were covered with dust, and she knew the sweat on her face was also making black lines in the layers of dirt.

"Everything here is fine," she said. "I was about to check to see if I could draw enough power from the emergency field to connect to an outside camera, if any are still out there."

Folle had turned and was holding on to the back of her chair. "Good idea," he said. "Let me—" He started to push off from the chair to move to the emergency power panel on the far wall when suddenly his entire body started to shimmer.

The shocked look on his face told Prescott that she wasn't imagining the effect. His entire body really was shimmering, as if she were looking at him through a layer of water and someone was stirring the water up.

Then he was gone.

No noise.

No pop.

Nothing.

Gone.

One moment he was there and the next moment he wasn't.

"Folle?" she said, starting toward his last position out of instinct.

He was gone.

She stopped, holding on to the back of her chair. Maybe her mind was gone as well. The guilt and stress of the last few weeks would have driven anyone insane. Why would she think she'd be any different?

"Folle?" she called out once more, only to have her voice echo through the empty chamber. Was this what happened when people died? Did the billions of people who were alive when the waves hit remain in place for a few moments, a few days, and then shimmer into nothingness?

Or had she imagined him in the first place? Maybe he hadn't come at all.

"You're starting to lose it," she said to the emptiness. "Hang in there just a little longer."

Long enough to find him. He had to be on the station somewhere. And if he wasn't, well, then maybe she would have to examine his disappearance as a death.

Another death caused by the experiment.

She gripped her chair, about to push herself toward the door, when the station started to rumble and shake.

Several chunks of steel fell from the ceiling. Dust floated around her. The emergency lights flickered.

And she knew she was going to die.

She swung around into her chair and held on. Every since she had followed Folle's advice, her survival instincts had kicked in. She didn't want to die.

Not anymore.

Even though she really didn't deserve to live.

Then the rumbling stopped and the dust began to settle again, coating her and everything in the room with another fine layer of gray.

In front of her the blank screens taunted her, laughed at her, told her by their very emptiness that she wasn't dead. Yet.

Inside, she was still shaking. Folle's disappearance terrified her more than she wanted to admit. She had spent the last five years with him on this research facility. They had been together most of that time.

He was helping her through this, and she had thought they would die together.

She brushed a strand of hair out of her face with her wrist lamp, its plastic cool against her forehead, and forced herself to take a deep breath. She didn't know he was dead yet. She had to search first.

She was a scientist. Scientists waited for evidence.

She hadn't touched him when he was here the last time. She had been working. She had been under a lot of strain. People who were under stress imagined things.

Like that odd feeling all over her body, as if something very small were breathing on her skin.

All of her skin.

She brought her arm down, and stared at it. It was composed of multicolored light. And it was shimmering.

She opened her mouth to call for help when—

—everything went black.

Then almost instantly, she was in bright light. She blinked. The air was clear here, and it smelled fresh.

"Captain," said a strange voice with an even stranger accent. "I've got one more set to go."

She blinked again. Red and green spots danced in her vision.

"Excellent, Scotty. Do it quickly. I'd like to be out of here as soon as possible." The second voice had a tinny quality and a completely different accent, another one she had never heard before.

Slowly the glare eased and she could see. She was standing on a platform with several circles on it. Directly across from her a man in a red uniform stood behind a console. He grinned at her, an infectious twinkle in his eyes. His skin was pale, and his hair was a shade of black she had never seen before.

Two other red-uniformed people stood beside an open door. Beyond it was a yellow corridor.

She swallowed and glanced at her arm— surreptitiously, she hoped. It was normal, as dust-covered as it had been in the main control room. Then she saw movement beside her. On the platform, three other members of her staff stood. She could have sworn they weren't there when she first arrived.

"And that's the last of them," the man said. He spoke loudly, as if he were addressing someone else. But the people at the door were staring straight ahead, like guards, and no one else appeared to be in the room.

Except Folle, standing in the shadows to her left.

"Folle," she said, breathing his name like a lifeline.

Scotty grinned, stepped forward, and held out his hand to help her down from the platform. "Welcome to the *Starship Enterprise*," he said.

Chapter Eleven

THE *ENTERPRISE* SWUNG out of the debris field left from the breakup of the fifth planet and its moon. Kirk let his grip on his chair relax slightly. Taking a starship twisting and weaving in through a thousand floating mountains, all moving in different directions at different speeds, was not his idea of excitement.

However, he couldn't contain his elation. They had rescued the survivors. Scotty had pulled them from their asteroid tomb, and they would be able to go on with their lives.

Very different lives from the ones they had before, but lives just the same.

Still, he couldn't let the elation overtake him. The *Enterprise* wasn't out of this mess yet.

The slowly forming rings surrounding the Tautee

sun stretched out on the viewscreen. Kirk felt like he was staring out over the top of a desert waste-land. Such devastation, and it had happened so quickly.

"Take us back to the *Farragut*'s position, Mister Sulu. As quickly as you safely can."

"Aye, sir." The strain of manually maneuvering around the huge asteroids had formed tiny exhaustion lines around Sulu's eyes. Still, his concentration never seemed to waver. At moments like this Kirk was very proud of his crew.

"Both Klingon vessels are still following us," Chekov said, almost sneering in disgust.

"Let them," Kirk said. The Klingon shadows annoyed him, too. "As long as they stay out of the way."

"Captain?" Spock said. He had an odd note in his voice.

Kirk glanced at him. Spock never showed elation—he rarely showed any emotion at all—but Kirk had learned to read the subtle nuances in Spock's inflections.

Kirk didn't like the sound of this one.

He swiveled his chair to make sure he could see his science officer clearly. For a moment he almost thought he saw a troubled expression on Spock's face, then dismissed the idea. Spock looked as impassive as always.

"I have been scanning a few of the larger aster-oids in the rings created after the breakup of the four inhabited planets."

"Looking for survivors," Kirk said, feeling an odd fluttering sensation in his stomach. He wanted to find more survivors, wanted the destruction to be less serious than it seemed.

But he also knew that the *Enterprise* and the *Farragut* had serious limitations in the rescue effort, and if more survivors were out there, they would need to be pulled off those asteroids immediately.

"I have found six other possible pockets of survivors," Spock said. "The survivors would seem to be in underground bunkers on larger asteroids. Based on these observations, I believe there may be as many as a dozen more bunkers and cavities filled with survivors among the asteroids."

A dozen more. They had rescued almost one hundred people off this one. The *Enterprise* barely had room for them.

Kirk pushed himself out of his chair, and hurried toward the science station. He leaned over the console, but saw no numbers. As usual, Spock had done the calculations in his head.

"Are you sure?" Kirk asked.

Spock's long face suddenly seemed even longer. He raised one eyebrow as if he couldn't believe that the captain had questioned him.

"Absolutely, Captain," Spock said.

"But at these distances, Mister Spock, how can you get accurate readings?" Chekov asked the question from his post near the screen.

Uhura was watching them.

Sulu had his head cocked, so that he could keep an eye on his work while monitoring the conversation.

They all understood the risks behind finding new survivors.

"At these distances," Spock said, in his slow, pedantic, I-cannot-believe-anyone-would-ask-this-question voice, "and with these subspace disturbances, I cannot get actual readings of humanoid forms."

"Oh," Kirk said.

Spock glanced around, and when no one else said a word, he continued. "However, I have searched the asteroids for such places as the bunker we just found, places that would hold atmosphere, and would sustain life since the planets' breakup. We must also calculate the incalculable factors as well. We found a moon base. I am looking at the planets only. We must assume there are other moon bases, and perhaps even a spaceship or two which survived unscathed. We—"

"How many survivors?" Kirk asked. He had grown tired of the explanation. He wanted to know what was before him. He wanted to know what decisions he faced next.

"I cannot give you a precise figure," Spock said.

Kirk groaned.

Spock pressed on. "There are too many variables. But the survivors of this incident may number in the thousands, possibly more."

"The thousands, possibly more." Kirk said, repeating Spock's words, not believing his ears.

He took a step backward. His stomach ached, and his mind swirled.

"Thousands?"

"Yes, Captain," Spock said. "Thousands."

Kirk staggered to his chair, and sat down. Between the *Farragut* and the *Enterprise*, they might be able to rescue five hundred.

But thousands were not possible without help.

A lot of help.

"Captain," Spock said. "Time is of the essence. With every subspace wave, the threat to these survivors grows."

"I know, Spock." Kirk took a deep breath. The main screen displayed the *Farragut* and four Klingon cruisers. Even if the Klingons deigned to help them, there wouldn't be enough room on the ships for thousands of survivors. The Federation had to send more ships.

But he didn't know if they would.

The Prime Directive. Admiral Hoffman's warning came back clearly to his mind.

Rescuing a few hundred survivors of a subwarp culture was one thing, but rescuing thousands and thousands would, through an odd twist of fate, violate the Prime Directive.

The Prime Directive stated that cultures had to live without interference from more advanced peoples. That allowed the cultures to develop at their own pace. Part of that development for many cultures, including Earth's, meant flirting with their own destruction. Famine, flood, and war threatened each culture at various times. It was natural.

The Federation could save the remaining hundred or so of a race because the culture was effectively dead. But to beam up thousands meant that this pre-warp culture would continue and suddenly learn about the existence of starships and warp drive and humans and Vulcans and Klingons.

Saving thousands meant violating the Prime Directive.

It meant a direct involvement in lives that should have no involvement at all.

The Federation had discovered the hard way that it was better to let the race suffer through its own natural existence—whatever that might be—than to interfere.

But in this case, the "natural existence" meant certain death for thousands.

He couldn't let thousands die.

But he didn't really have a choice. His orders were that he had to.

Chapter Twelve

BRUISES, CUTS, BROKEN BONES.

And filth.

McCoy hadn't seen that much filth since he went back in time to old Earth. Although these people couldn't be blamed for the dirt. They had lived for weeks in a crisis situation.

McCoy was working in the cargo decks. The hundred survivors fit better in here than they did in sickbay. Security was carrying the worst of the wounded—those with shattered limbs, gangrenous infections—to sickbay, where Nurse Chapel would sedate them until McCoy could get there.

Fortunately he had found no internal injuries yet. And even more fortunately, Scotty's golf contraption was disassembled. Instead of fake green grass and mist off the sea, the deck had been transformed into a makeshift hospital and refugee area full of beds, blankets, and wounded.

Tauteeans leaned against walls, and lay, eyes closed, on beds. A few sat on chairs, their short legs unable to reach the ground. They didn't look like children, though. They looked like shrunken humans.

But they weren't human.

Tauteeans were a thin-boned, almost birdlike people. He doubted that the heaviest of them weighed more than a normal ten-year-old child. The men were no more than five feet tall, and the women were shorter than that. But they had a compelling attractiveness that had something to do with their frailty, and with their delicate bodies. Something that made McCoy want to protect them.

Maybe it was the sense of despair around them.

McCoy had been on rescue missions before, and the survivors always celebrated when they were lifted away from certain death. Then, days—sometimes months—later, they felt survivors' guilt. But these people seemed to be feeling it already. Even the ones who weren't seriously wounded closed their eyes and didn't speak much to those around them.

The silence in the bays was unnerving. His voice, blended with that of his current patient, would bounce against the high ceiling, sending mocking echoes throughout.

No one looked, no one watched, not even to see if a colleague was all right. Not even after a subspace wave hit, and they all clutched the nearest post, the nearest wall, for balance.

McCoy would have to monitor all of his patients carefully. Despair this deep made a shallow cut deadly; he had learned long ago that people who wished to die often could force their bodies to cease functioning properly.

In fact, he was more worried about their mental conditions than their physical ones. The loss of a house, a dwelling, a plot of land, was bad enough. The loss of a country was devastating. The loss of a planet, and the destruction of a solar system, was beyond his comprehension.

Not only was the beloved dwelling gone, but so were the land that it rested on and the air that surrounded it. He hadn't returned to his family home, his Earth, in a long time, but if he received news that Earth and her sister planets were gone— well, the thought made his breath catch in his throat.

McCoy was working on a man who had cuts all over his hands and arms. One long gash ran down the side of his cheek, and bumps rose from his forehead as if he had been hit with a dozen rocks. The cuts were dirty but not yet infected. McCoy shot the man full of antibiotics and gingerly picked up the man's left hand. McCoy was leery of these fine bones. If he gripped them too hard, he felt he would shatter them with his simple touch.

The man had moaned once, when McCoy touched a particularly deep slash in the upper arm, and then had said nothing else. His breathing sounded loud in the cargo bay's stillness.

Then McCoy heard a chair clang. He glanced to his left, past the rows of barrels that Scotty kept for some unknown purpose, and watched a slender dark-haired woman move from person to person. She touched each Tauteean she passed, and spoke softly. They smiled in response. Sad smiles, but smiles nonetheless.

The woman moved with both leadership and apology, as if she were accepting responsibility for everything. McCoy had seen Jim Kirk do the same in difficult situations. The leadership seemed to give the others strength, and the apology was an acknowledgment of their pain.

McCoy smiled to himself and went back to his work. Her low voice soothed even him. Her touch with these people would probably help them more than McCoy could.

He had finished with the man's arms and had just reached for the long gash when he felt a presence beside him. McCoy looked down. The woman was running her fingers over the man's healed skin.

"Be careful," McCoy said. "It'll still be a bit tender."

She looked up at him, her dark eyes intense and shadowed at the same time. "It looks healed," she said. Her voice was rich, deep, and musical.

"It is," McCoy said. "But the memory of the pain remains for about an hour."

A man came up behind her. He was as tall as she was. He put a hand possessively on her shoulder. She didn't shrug him off, but she didn't acknowledge him either. The man didn't seem to mind.

She watched for another minute, then seemed to gather herself. She obviously hadn't come to talk about the wounded. She had come for something else.

McCoy finished cleaning the gash, then pinched its edges together and mended the skin. The other man gasped—obviously this technology was beyond them—but the woman didn't. She waited until McCoy was finished.

He glanced down at her, and she lifted her chin, clearly ready to ask her question.

"I would like to speak to your . . ." The woman hesitated for a moment before finding the right word. ". . . captain. Is there some way you can help me do this?"

Suddenly the ship rocked and shuddered as another subspace wave crashed into it. The room seemed to rumble, and people fought to keep their feet. McCoy spread his feet and managed to remain standing over his patient out of almost sheer will. The woman in front of him also remained standing, while the man following her was knocked to the deck. Screams and cries resounded against the walls as wounds were reopened, and people fell.

McCoy also sensed an undercurrent of deep fear. These people were afraid the subspace waves would kill them. They had a right to be afraid.

And all reacted accordingly. All except this alien woman beside him. She withstood the shuddering and shaking of the deck as if it were only a passing annoyance and not important in the scheme of things.

Almost as quickly as it hit, the shuddering

passed. The cries stopped, and the silence returned. The woman was still looking at him as if they hadn't been interrupted.

McCoy cleared his throat. "The captain is pretty busy at the moment, as you might guess. I can take you to him later when things are calmer."

"I think your captain will want to see me," the woman said. "I am the leader of these people. I also have information that might be helpful about the shock waves."

McCoy nodded and glanced around. This room was under control. The survivors in the other cargo bay weren't as badly injured as the folks here. He needed to go to sickbay, to mend the broken bones and work on the serious infections, but he could take a detour to the bridge. It wouldn't take long, and it might turn out interesting.

"All right," he said. "I'm sure the captain would appreciate the help. I'll take you to him." He put out his hand. "I'm Dr. Leonard McCoy."

The woman hesitated for a moment, then put her surprisingly small hand in his, like a queen at a Regency ball. "Prescott," she said, and, indicating the man behind her, added, "This is Folle."

McCoy nodded at her companion, and resisted the urge to bow over her hand like a courtly gentleman. Her strength attracted him, but her fragility and sense of loss made him protective. The man watched him warily.

McCoy reluctantly released her hand.

She was studying his face with puzzlement.

"Have I done something to offend you?" he asked, suddenly worried that touching hands might have a different significance in her culture than it did in his.

She shook her head. "Dr. Leonard McCoy, why do you have three names?"

McCoy opened his mouth, closed it, and opened it again. Why did he have three names? He suddenly couldn't think of a good answer.

She watched him with a seriousness that made him feel as if his life depended on his answer.

Finally he just laughed and said, "My people have never been known for doing anything the easy way."

Her puzzled frown kept him chuckling to himself all the way to the turbolift.

Chapter Thirteen

THE BRIDGE OF THE *Enterprise* was as silent as a tomb.

It felt as if time had stopped.

Uhura held a hand over her communications console.

Sulu was still watching the screen, but his head was tilted oddly as if he were trying to see the captain out of the corner of his eye.

Chekov *was* watching him, eyes wide.

The three other ensigns on the bridge had swiveled their chairs so that they could see the captain.

And Spock was studying him as if he were a particularly interesting—and possibly dangerous—extraterrestrial bug.

Kirk was used to the scrutiny, and he appreciated the silence. He had to decide whether or not to rescue the remaining survivors of the Tautee disaster—and how.

Spock said there might be thousands.

Thousands were more than the *Enterprise* and *Farragut* could handle. And with that many survivors of a pre-warp culture, a rescue attempt would be violating the Prime Directive, and the Federation would no doubt order him to back off if he asked for more help.

But there had to be a way around the rules. He had beaten the *Kobayashi Maru* and he could beat this.

On the main screen in front of him the four Klingon cruisers hung. They seemed to be just waiting also. But why and for what, Kirk had no idea.

Maybe the Klingons were the key to solving the survivors' problem. Kirk swiveled around to face his science officer. "Spock, any theory as to what caused this destruction?"

Spock raised an eyebrow as if that were not what he expected the captain to ask. "I have no concrete theory yet, Captain. I do not know what caused the destruction. It may have been caused by the Tauteeans. It may have been a natural disaster of a type we have not seen before. I just do not know, and at this moment I am unwilling to speculate."

"You could have just said no," Kirk muttered.

Spock swiveled, and glanced into his scope.

Kirk steepled his fingers. Thousands of lives rested on this next decision.

Of course, his old colleague and nemesis, Admiral William Banning, would have said that Kirk did not trust the process well enough. The Federation's guidelines were simple: A pre-warp culture had to develop naturally. If a natural disaster wiped it out, then that was part of "naturally." If a natural disaster hit, and only a few survived, they needed the opportunity to save themselves without help.

But Kirk wasn't convinced this disaster was natural. And the Federation had no real guidelines for what to do with the pre-warp survivors of an attack by a more advanced race.

"Captain," Spock said, his voice calm as always. "Another subspace wave shall hit us in ten seconds."

"Could a Klingon superweapon have caused all this?" Kirk asked.

Spock glanced over his shoulder at the captain. Uhura took a deep, sudden breath and held it.

Out of the corner of his eye Kirk could see Sulu turn to look at him.

"At this point, Captain," Spock said carefully, "I am not willing to speculate."

The entire ship shook and moaned as the internal stabilizers fought to keep the ship level against the huge forces shaking it. Kirk held on to the arms of his chair and rode it out. The chair bumped against his spine and legs, the thin cushion no protection against each impact.

Sulu clung to the helm.

Chekov tried to swivel his chair back and nearly fell again.

And Uhura maintained her balance with the grace of a ballerina.

They were getting used to these waves, although this one felt as if it was bumping harder than the last.

Spock frowned and even before the shaking had stopped turned back to his scope. Kirk jumped to his feet, relieved to be off that chair, and moved up to the rail near the science station.

"Was that more intense?" he asked. He already knew the answer. It was clearly a stronger wave, but he needed Spock to confirm his senses.

After a moment Spock looked up. "Since our arrival into this system, the intensity of the subspace wave has increased by almost ten percent. The rate of increase appears to be constant."

"Constant?" Kirk said. He had not expected that. He had thought that all the waves had been similar until this one. "Can you speculate on this increase, Spock?"

"Unfortunately, yes, Captain," Spock said. "If this rate of increase continues, the Tautee sun will be torn apart in approximately twenty-seven-point-three days."

"Torn completely apart?" Kirk asked. He couldn't wrap his mind around that level of destruction any more than he could around fifteen planets destroyed.

Spock nodded. "Yes, sir. In sixty-two days the closest planetary system will be destroyed."

Kirk could feel his stomach starting to flutter, and he took a deep breath. It didn't seem to help. There were four billion more lives in the Wheaten system. "It will spread that far?" Kirk asked, his voice low, hoping he had heard wrong.

Spock kept one hand on the science console, as if he were still bracing himself against the subspace wave. "If the rate of increase continues, and I see no logical reason why it should not, the waves emanating from this rift in space will be strong enough to destroy the planet Vulcan in approximately four hundred and eight days. And the planet Earth twenty-six days later."

"Four hundred and eight days?"

Kirk leaned against the rail. Its support felt good against his back. Klingons, survivors, the Prime Directive, and now this. They would have to close that rift somehow, stop the waves. One year and the Federation would cease to exist if he didn't act. He had to stop those waves.

And he would wager the only way to stop the waves was to know what caused them.

Kirk turned again to face Spock. "If these waves are growing in intensity, Mr. Spock, how long until we have to move the *Enterprise?*"

"Ten hours, Captain. I would recommend, however, that we find a safer distance before that."

Kirk returned to his chair, and sat heavily in it, instantly regretting the movement as a jolt ran up his spine. Ten hours. Why did every important event in his career have to have such a short timetable?

He glanced at the Klingon ships on the screen.

Suddenly rescuing Tautee survivors and violating the Prime Directive seemed very small. If he didn't act and act now, there would be no Prime Directive, no Federation, and no planet Earth.

The whir of the turbolift doors filled the silence on the bridge. He didn't turn to see who had entered. He had too much on his plate already. The next problem, whatever it was, could wait.

The bridge crew seemed to feel the same way, for no one—except Sulu—had taken their gaze off him. They were waiting for him to act.

And act he would.

He clenched a fist and pushed it into the armrest. "How do we close this rift in space, Mister Spock?"

"I do not know, Captain. I do not even know how it was created."

"I do, Captain."

Kirk didn't recognize the voice.

He spun quickly around to face Dr. McCoy and tiny people who were obviously two of the Tautee survivors. The man was staring at the equipment in awe. He was small and delicate, looking more like a boy than a full-grown being, except for the age lines on his face.

The woman was staring at Kirk, her chin up. She was the one who had spoken.

She was clearly the one in charge of the Tautee survivors. Even though she was built as slightly as the man, Kirk would never mistake her for a teenager. Her clothes were ripped and tattered and her face and arms covered with dirt, yet she had the bearing and strength of someone who had been in command a long, long time.

"You know what happened?" he asked.

The woman moved forward around the railing and down until she stood in front of Kirk as if he were her judge. He looked down at her.

"My name is Prescott," she said in a full, rich voice. "I caused all this destruction."

Chapter Fourteen

"SIR, WE CANNOT TELL what they beamed aboard."

KerDaq glared across the war-darkened bridge at KobtaH. Bits of smoke still filled the air from the ruined control panel near the door. One of his officers had fallen into it during a subspace wave. Although KerDaq's back had been turned at the time, he doubted the damaged panel was an accident. He suspected that the officer had been pushed. He had been rising too quickly, and KerDaq had been favoring him of late.

Such favoritism always set the officer up for attack. The officer who could defend himself was the only officer who rose beyond his station.

Which brought KerDaq back to the problem that faced him now. "You cannot?" He asked his science officer.

"No, sir."

KerDaq scowled. He should cut the man into pieces like the planets of this system. How could he not know if the humans had beamed their super-weapon aboard? How could such incompetence exist?

Especially on his ship.

"What *could* you identify?" He deliberately let his voice fill with sarcasm. "Are you even certain that they transported something aboard?"

"Yes, Commander," KobtaH said. "They staged several large beam-outs from the center of that asteroid."

"Several?" KerDaq asked.

"Yes, Commander."

"You had several chances and still you do not know?"

"I assumed it was the superweapon, sir."

"You assumed. You *assumed.* You did not check."

KobtaH bared his teeth. He knew that KerDaq was questioning his competence. If KerDaq continued to do so, the man's position would soon be available to someone more competent.

The rest of the bridge crew turned to watch the interchange.

"Did you?" KerDaq stood, fingers tight against the palm of his hand, the spikes on his gloves catching the dim light. "You did not check."

"No, Commander. But something of that size, and taking that many beam-outs, could only be the superweapon."

KerDaq took a step closer to KobtaH. There

would be no way to check now. KobtaH's incompetence had cost them knowledge. "You had better ask the protection of Kahless in case you are wrong."

"I am not wrong, Commander," KobtaH said.

KerDaq squinted at him. KobtaH was shorter, his ridges smoother, but he had power, and connections. KerDaq was not ready to discard him yet. Besides, he believed that for all of KobtaH's incompetence, KobtaH was correct.

What else could induce Kirk to travel into the middle of those subspace waves? This story of survivors was a faulty cover. No air-breathing creature could survive a disaster of this magnitude.

KerDaq grunted and returned to his command chair.

He swiveled it, and leaned forward, glad it was raised, glad that it made him seem even more powerful than he was. "So you believe they are ready to leave with their weapon?"

"I don't think so, Supreme Commander."

KerDaq smiled. KobtaH only used his official title when he was worried about KerDaq's reaction. They had served a long time together and KerDaq had seen that pattern before.

"Upon what facts do you base your opinion?"

KobtaH glanced around. The others were watching him, waiting to see how KerDaq would punish him for such disastrous errors.

KobtaH stood alone. No one came to his rescue, and no one would.

He straightened his shoulders, accepting his potential fate like a good Klingon, and took a deep breath. "I base my opinion upon this, sir. The subspace waves are still increasing in power."

"They are, huh?" KerDaq spoke as if he had expected that answer. But he had not. KobtaH had surprised him. And KobtaH had found one of the few things that would convince anyone.

KerDaq's silence seemed to make KobtaH nervous. "At this rate of increase," KobtaH added, "this sun will be destroyed in a very few days at most."

"And destroy the remaining evidence." KerDaq growled.

He swiveled his chair back into position and glared at the screen. On it, the debris from the destroyed planets formed quarter circles around the sun. The Federation ships looked small and evil against that backdrop.

The Federation's trickery was suddenly very clear. They had come here, tested their weapon, retrieved what the information they needed from the test and then set the superweapon to destroy the sun. And in the process the weapon and all the evidence would also be destroyed.

Kirk had probably not beamed aboard the weapon, but the data.

"Brilliant," KerDaq said to himself. This was Federation trickery on an unparalleled scale. And if they could destroy a remote star system like Tautee in less than a week, then they could do the same to the Klingon Empire—or any other system that offended them.

The Klingons needed the information on this weapon. They needed to know how to defend themselves, how to prevent any more destruction of this kind.

"Inform the other commanders to follow my lead," he said. "I want the *Enterprise* captured, not destroyed."

"But Commander, they have—"

"They have information vital to the survival of the Klingon Empire," KerDaq said. "We shall learn it. All of it."

KobtaH grinned.

The other officers growled their approval.

KerDaq gripped the arms of his chair and leaned forward. "On my signal," he said, "we will attack."

"Captain," Science Officer Richard Lee said, his voice suddenly holding a bit of panic in it. "The Klingons are powering up their weapons and raising shields."

"Red alert," Bogle said. "Hail the *Enterprise.*"

As if Kirk wouldn't have noticed. Not likely, but it was better to take no chances. He'd play this one exactly by the book.

Bogle ran a hand through his thinning hair. Too much had been happening too quickly. His bridge crew, hunched over their consoles, could barely keep track of things. He suspected Kirk's were the same way.

Bogle believed in the Prime Directive, believed in it more than he believed in any other aspect of the Federation. Saving one hundred survivors could be squeezed past the Prime Directive, just barely.

But thousands, as Kirk had informed him might

still be in those rocks, could not. And as much as it bothered his conscience, he understood the reasons behind it. Laws applied in difficult circumstances, painful circumstances, as well as easy ones. They could not save those survivors.

Yet Bogle knew Kirk. He knew Kirk would search for a way around this. If Kirk found that way, it had to be within Federation guidelines or Bogle would not agree to it. In fact, he would be forced to stop Kirk, and he didn't want that situation to happen.

Then there was this business about the expanding waves, expanding so far that they would threaten the Federation's home systems. Bogle shook his head. More than enough for any commander to consider.

He had been thinking about those things, not about the Klingons.

"I have Captain Kirk, sir," Gustavus said.

"Put him on screen." Bogle rested his arms on his captain's chair and leaned toward the viewscreen. He wanted to look at ease, even though he was not.

Kirk, on the other hand, looked tense. And as if he were thriving on the increased adrenaline. Behind him red lights flashed. The *Enterprise* was also on red alert.

"Do you have any idea what they're up to?" Bogle asked.

"Knowing the Klingons," Kirk said, "it could be anything. And their timing is typical too. I've been hailing them and they're not responding."

"Do you think I should try?"

Kirk shook his head. "If he's not responding to me, he won't respond to you."

"What have we done?" Bogle asked.

"Maybe nothing," Kirk said. "Maybe we're too close to something they're protecting."

"A weapon?" Bogle had hoped this destruction wasn't caused by a superweapon. He just didn't want to believe that was possible.

"Perhaps," Kirk said, "Or perhaps they've just decided they don't like us anymore. We'll just have to ride this one out."

Bogle nodded. "We'll guard your back."

"We'll do the same for you," Kirk said. "Kirk out."

The screen went dark for half a second.

"Gustavus!" Bogle said. "I want to see those Klingons."

"Aye, sir," she said. The screen came back on, showing four gray Klingon battle cruisers against the slowly growing Rings of Tautee.

"Sir," Lee said, "they're moving."

And as he spoke, the ships split apart from each other, and moved into attack formation.

Bogle stood so quickly his chair spun. "Arm photon torpedoes and phasers and stand ready."

Two of the cruisers peeled away and moved in a quick arching circle high above the two starships.

"Those two are making a run at us," Lee said.

"Wait until they fire the first shot," Bogle said. He didn't want to be accused of starting a war between the Federation and the Klingons.

Even though his heart was racing, he felt quite calm. Now that he knew what the Klingons were up to, he could counter. He might not have spent much time with Klingons, but he knew how to fight them. "Then return fire. Pattern Alpha."

He sat down in his command chair and braced himself. The few long seconds before the Klingon ships began firing seemed to stretch into a lifetime. His lifetime and maybe many others.

His ship rocked with the impact. His officers, braced as they were, simply moved with the ship. Hands moved so rapidly he could barely see them. And then, across the darkened screen, a volley of photon torpedoes streaked red as they headed toward the two battle cruisers.

The battle was engaged and Bogle didn't even know what they were fighting about.

And he really doubted Jim Kirk did either.

All he knew was that if all the races and people in this sector were to survive, including the Klingons, the Federation had to win this fight.

And they had to win it fast.

Chapter Fifteen

PRESCOTT CLUNG TO the railing on the balcony encircling the ship's command center. Her fingers barely fit around the cool, unfamiliar surface. Everything was big here, and powerful, and noisy.

The pulsating red lights were accompanied by a blare that the alien crew didn't seem to notice. The ship rocked and bounced from what she had first thought were subspace waves, and gradually began to realize was another ship firing upon them.

Her mind was overloaded, her body rigid with shock. She was coasting along the surface of things when actually everything she had ever believed was being shattered, much as her own experiments had shattered her home.

She didn't doubt that now. Perhaps she could

accept it because she was here, in this magical place, with these extraordinary aliens.

They looked Tauteean, but they were big like giants from the ancient mythologies. The men had twice the height and girth of Folle, but they carried it well, with muscle not fat.

The women were large too, and muscular, as if they could fight every bit as well as their men. And even though they seemed to know her language perfectly, they spoke it with varying accents— some musical, as in the case of the man who had brought them to the *Enterprise,* and some harsh, like Dr. Leonard McCoy's.

Somehow she preferred Dr. Leonard McCoy's accent.

He was standing on one side of her, clutching the rail too. Only his long fingers wrapped around it, and he moved with the rhythm of the ship as if he had been born to it.

The others did as well, and she wondered where they had been born, how they came here, and what they were. They didn't seem to belong to the same race. The rail-thin man with the greenish skin seemed particularly unusual. His ears, his eyebrows, and his skin tone marked him as different, but his attitude was what made him seem especially alien. While the other members of the crew rocked and worked and muttered to themselves, he kept his balance and his composure.

Prescott watched them all, feeling absurdly detached. It was as if her mind had separated from her body. After all the misery she had felt on the destroyed moon, it felt odd not to feel anything at all. Her scientific brain told her that she felt nothing because she had already given herself up for dead. When that explanation felt lame, her brain told her that she felt nothing because she was in shock.

But deep down, she actually believed she felt nothing because she had already lost everything of meaning. Losing her life was just a detail, and a minor one at that.

Folle stood on her other side, looking as numb as she felt. He was having trouble keeping his balance. As the ship rocked, he occasionally slammed into her, muttering an apology every time. Finally she picked up one hand and placed it on his. Dr. Leonard McCoy watched the movement with interest.

No one else was looking at them.

Captain James Kirk had taken what appeared to be his normal seat in the middle of the command center, his attention never wavering from the huge screen in front of his two crew.

The screen showed space. She recognized the growing rings, the distant sun, and the remains of the Tautee system. Her home. But smack in the middle of the screen were two gray ships shaped like Ne Lizards, with large heads, sleek backs, and wings. These, apparently, were the enemy, the Cling-Ons.

She wondered at the name, and hoped it wasn't some type of attack. It would make them even more like the Ne Lizards; once they contacted the skin, they stuck.

Another ship was flanked by two gray vessels.

The other ship, which looked like a saucer with a tail, was apparently Captain James Kirk's ally, *Farragut.*

So much information, so much was happening, and she had no real way to make sense of it all.

But she did know that the red streaks that appeared on the screen were the weapons. She learned that by watching one streak toward the screen. A second later, the ship rocked with impact.

"Shields holding, sir," the large man with the almost indecipherable accent said.

"Return fire, Mister Chekov," Captain James Kirk said.

Streaks of light seemed to originate beyond the screen. They grew smaller as they headed toward the gray vessels, then exploded in orange balls near the vessels' sides.

"Direct hit," Mister Chekov said, balling his fist.

"Continue firing." Captain James Kirk looked as if he were fighting the fight with his bare hands. He moved constantly, leaning forward, leaning back, watching each member of his crew. At the moment, he swiveled his chair, and looked at the greenish man. "How's the *Farragut* doing?

"They are firing upon two of the cruisers," the greenish man said. He sounded as calm as he looked. "They do not seem to have sustained any damage."

"Good." Captain James Kirk stood and stepped away from his chair. He stopped behind the other large man, who had stared at the screen continually. "Mister Sulu, take us directly at KerDaq's ship."

"Aye, sir." Mister Sulu had a deep soothing voice. Of all the alien crew, he was the only one who sounded the most Tauteean.

Prescott could not feel the ship turn, but the view on screen changed, sweeping away from the gray vessels, and then suddenly toward one. Bursts of red fire appeared against the darkness of space.

Dr. Leonard McCoy's grip tightened on the railing. He had been making small snorting noises, disapproving noises, for some time now. Finally, as the ship appeared to bear down on the gray vessel, he muttered, "This is just plain stupid."

Captain James Kirk whirled. "You have an opinion, Bones?"

"I always have an opinion, Jim," Dr. Leonard McCoy said. "I think we're getting a little sidetracked here."

"We didn't start this, Bones." Captain James Kirk sounded testy.

"Well, I wish we'd hurry up and end it."

"So do I, Bones," the captain said. He turned back to stare at the screen.

The two ships seemed to pass within touching distance of each other on the screen, and again the *Enterprise* was rocked as enemy fire pounded it. Prescott could not imagine the force and strength of these ships and these weapons. Races that could travel between the stars like this must obviously have very, very powerful weapons.

"Captain," Mister Chekov said, "the shields are at eighty percent."

"Captain," the green-skinned man said without

giving Captain James Kirk a chance to respond to Mister Chekov, "we have a very strong subspace wave in fifty seconds. With our weakened shields, we will feel this blast more intensely than we did the others."

"Are we in danger, Mister Spock?" Captain James Kirk asked.

"Are you referring to the shields, the Klingons, the subspace wave, or all three, Captain?"

"A simple yes or no would have done fine, Spock," Dr. Leonard McCoy said.

"Doctor," the greenish man—Spock? one name only?—said, "in order to answer an inquiry precisely it is necessary to understand—"

"The shields and the wave, Spock," Captain James Kirk snapped. "Yes or no?"

"Of course, Captain," Spock said. "A wave of that intensity combined with lower shields would—"

"Shields at seventy percent," Mister Chekov said, his voice holding an edge of worry that even Prescott could hear. She thought it ironic. Rescued from certain death only to be killed with her rescuers in a war she didn't even understand.

More blasts rocked the ship. It felt as if Prescott's fingers had dug grooves into the odd material of the rail.

"Spock." Captain James Kirk bounded up the stairs, stopping just behind Prescott. "Is the subspace wave coming directly out of the debris from the ninth planet?"

"Yes, Captain," Spock said as if they were discussing lunch. "I suggest we ride with the wave again to reduce the strain on our weakened shields."

They were operating on a level that was so far above Prescott that she felt like a child around adults. The height difference didn't help. They thought they could ride out these waves of destruction, survive them with minimal damage. That concept alone startled her to the very core of her being. These waves had destroyed her homeworld and every planet in her system. How could this ship just ride them and escape damage? What amazing power these aliens had.

Captain James Kirk nodded. His energy was infectious. Prescott could feel it beside her like a barely contained fusion reaction.

"Let's do this as we did it in the debris field," Captain James Kirk said. "Mister Spock, send the coordinates to Sulu's screen. But before you lay in Spock's course, Sulu, I want you to plot a course directly at the ninth planet and immediately engage at one-sixth impulse. Be prepared to reverse course and follow Mister Spock's directions on my mark."

"Aye, sir," Mister Sulu said.

Prescott had no idea what Captain James Kirk was planning, but obviously the crew did and they followed his directions without question. The man was clearly a very powerful and trusted leader.

Dr. Leonard McCoy just stood beside her, shaking his head. He hadn't let go of the railing either. She wondered if part of his impatience was due to his position in the command center. He had said he only wanted to make a quick stop here on the way to sickbay where, he said, more wounded waited for him.

Was that the sidetrack?

She wasn't sure. She wasn't even sure why these people sometimes used three names and sometimes used only one. She wasn't sure about anything anymore.

"Mister Chekov?" Captain James Kirk asked. Prescott didn't understand the question.

Mister Chekov nodded. "The Klingons are turning and following us."

Captain James Kirk smiled and sank into his command chair. He gripped the arms as if they were an extension of his own body.

"Fifteen seconds," Spock said.

"On my mark, Mister Sulu."

Mister Sulu nodded.

It seemed to Prescott that the entire alien crew was holding its breath.

The seconds stretched.

Even she found herself holding her breath, and she didn't know what they were doing. Or why.

Folle glanced at her, his eyes wide. His fingers were cold beneath hers.

"Now, Mister Sulu," Captain James Kirk said. "Reverse course."

"Five seconds," Spock said.

"Brace yourselves," Captain James Kirk shouted.

On the screen the two enemy ships flashed past just as the ship was hit with a rocking, tumbling, crashing sound. Prescott lost her grip on the rail and tumbled back against the wall. The jolt shuddered through her spine. She rolled with the force and came up sitting in time to see Folle slam against the wall beside her. He grunted audibly and then turned blue.

Two of the crew were also tossed from their seats, and in the back of Prescott's mind she wondered why, with such advance technology, they didn't have something as simple as seat belts.

Then the shaking and roaring stopped.

McCoy, who had managed to remain standing, quickly moved over and began examining Folle, all the while muttering to himself about all this being stupid.

"Damage reports on decks four, five, and seven," the large woman in the tiny red dress said as she held her hand to her ear. Her voice seemed level and almost calm.

"Shields are down to fifty percent, but they are still holding," Mister Chekov said.

"All stop," Captain James Kirk ordered.

Prescott felt the ship stop moving. It jerked noticeably, and she frowned. She hadn't thought such maneuvers were possible in space.

Captain James Kirk turned to Spock. "Did our friends make it?"

Spock stared into his scope for a moment, then spoke without looking up. "Both vessels have sustained heavy damage. KerDaq's ship has the most amount of damage. The second ship has no power."

"And Kelly's ship?"

Spock again spoke without looking up. "The

Farragut, possibly combined with that last wave, has inflicted heavy damage on a third ship. The remaining Klingon ship is moving to aid the other ship. All hostilities have stopped. Captain . . ."

Spock's voice trailed off as if he were studying his scope harder than normal. Then he continued, his voice level. "KerDaq's ship will sustain a core breach in less than a minute."

Without understanding what the words meant, even Prescott understood the implications of Spock's words. The crew on KerDaq's ship would soon die. And if she had understood correctly, none of the other enemy ships could help them.

She pushed herself upright. Even though she had never seen KerDaq, even though she knew nothing about his people, her heart went out to him. She had been in that position just a few hours ago.

Captain James Kirk punched a button on his chair without hesitation. "Transporter room. I want emergency beam-out of all personnel on the Klingon flagship. Security to transporter room on the double."

"Klingons, too, Jim?" Dr. Leonard McCoy asked. "Don't you think the ship's a bit crowded already?"

"Trust me, Bones." Captain James Kirk stood. Prescott had never seen such a restless man. He glanced at Spock and then grinned. Spock remained stoic, but raised a single eyebrow. The movement had the same effect as a smile.

Captain James Kirk laughed and turned back to the screen. Prescott followed his gaze. The two green vessels floated at odd angles, obviously damaged. Suddenly the one on the right seemed to collapse in on itself. Then it exploded in a bright flash of orange and red.

"We got them all, sir," said a tinny disembodied voice.

Captain James Kirk punched the comm button again. "Good work. Escort Commander KerDaq to the bridge. We have a few matters to discuss."

"Aye, sir," the tinny voice said.

Captain James Kirk then turned to Dr. Leonard McCoy and smiled. "Well, Bones, did I end that fast enough for you?"

Prescott glanced at McCoy.

McCoy snorted and kept working on Folle. "It would have been better not happening at all."

"I agree," Captain James Kirk said.

Then the captain turned and focused on Prescott where she leaned against the wall. "It seems we have a few minutes now," he said.

Beside her Folle moaned and McCoy helped him sit up.

Quickly, under his intense gaze, she scrambled to her feet and stepped forward. "I am Prescott, the leader of the group you rescued."

Kirk stood and bowed slightly. His gaze perused her, all of her, as if he were trying to assess all the differences between them in a single glance. "Captain James T. Kirk of the *U.S.S. Enterprise,*" he said. "Pleased to have you aboard."

She was stunned at how nice he seemed. After just fighting two enemy ships, he suddenly seemed warm and friendly.

Beside her McCoy stood. "She claims to be responsible for the destruction of this system."

"I heard her earlier, Bones," Captain James Kirk said, the warmth in his voice like a caress. Prescott put her hands behind her back. This man was as dangerous as he was unpredictable. And powerful. Very powerful.

"I simply don't believe it," he said.

She straightened her back, wishing for the first time in her life that she was taller. "Believe it," she said. "I destroyed the system. And if you give me a chance, I'll tell you how."

"And why," Captain James Kirk asked, "would you destroy your own system?"

"It was an accident." Her voice trembled and she forced herself to keep it level.

Everyone in the ship's command center stared at her.

And for the longest time no one said a word.

Chapter Sixteen

Kɪʀᴋ ғᴇʟᴛ ʜɪᴍsᴇʟғ ғʀᴇᴇᴢᴇ.

All the energy and excitement of the last few moments faded as he realized not just what the frail Tauteean woman had said, but what it meant.

She believed she had destroyed her entire race.

A shiver ran down his back. Whether or not she was right, he had to listen to her.

Spock had swiveled in his chair and was staring at her. Uhura took her hand away from her ear, her wide brown eyes soft with compassion. Sulu turned, mouth open. McCoy took a step forward, reached for the woman—Prescott—but let his hand fall a few inches away from her.

The Tauteean on the floor was breathing in deep shuddery breaths. He put a hand on the wall, and propelled himself upward, as if her words meant more than his pain.

"Prescott," he said, his voice shadowy with lack of oxygen.

"It's all right, Folle," she said, without even turning around.

Kirk frowned. He had been so convinced that the Klingons had caused this with a superweapon—and he still wasn't willing to rule that possibility out. But the possibility had diminished greatly, and he didn't need Spock's gift with percentages to tell him just how much.

But that didn't solve the problem from the other side. The Klingons had accused him of using a special weapon. He had thought it a cover for their own behavior, but what if they were both wrong, and this Prescott was right?

Kirk couldn't examine her evidence alone. He needed the Klingons here as well.

"Captain James Kirk," she said. "I will give you the answers you've been seeking."

He nodded, feeling a bit off balance from the new direction the conversation had gone. "Before you tell me," he said, "there's someone else who needs to hear this story. Let's wait until he gets here."

As if on cue the door to the turbolift whisked open and KerDaq emerged, flanked on both sides by security men. Next to the Tauteeans, KerDaq looked like a giant. He towered over Kirk. Prescott only came to his beltline.

KerDaq brushed her aside as he strode across the bridge, his gaze, fierce under his abnormally pronounced brow ridges, only on Kirk.

Kirk held KerDaq's gaze. Klingons bullied anyone weaker and they respected strength. Kirk could play the game, better than KerDaq would ever know.

"Why didn't you let us die in battle, like warriors?" KerDaq demanded, his voice full and angry. It rumbled through the bridge as if the *Enterprise* were too small to hold a Klingon presence.

Kirk noticed that Prescott stepped back, shocked, and almost afraid at the appearance of the huge, rough Klingon. Tauteean features were very similar to human features. She had been staring at Spock as if she had never seen anything like him. A Klingon must have seemed like something out of a nightmare.

"Your death would have served no purpose," Kirk said, keeping his voice loud and firm and strong. "I would have loved to blow your ship from space, but this time I can't claim credit for the explosion. The subspace wave destroyed your ship, not the *Enterprise.*"

"I know that, Kirk." KerDaq moved one step closer to Kirk. "You lured us into a trap."

KerDaq spat out the words.

Kirk resisted the urge to wipe the saliva from his face. Instead Kirk laughed. The laugh sounded forced and calculated to him, but KerDaq wouldn't know the difference.

KerDaq glowered.

Kirk's laugh became real. He had never induced *that* disgruntled an expression in a Klingon before. "You may be right about that." He pushed past KerDaq, brushing hard against KerDaq's shoulder, spinning the Klingon slightly around. Kirk knew KerDaq wouldn't attack him, at least not at the moment. Klingons were brutal and fearless warriors, but they were also smart. KerDaq would listen.

He had no other choice.

"This is Prescott," Kirk said, stopping near the small, thin woman, yet turning to face the Klingon. "She is a member of the race that inhabited this system."

"I do not care, Kirk. What has happened is between you and me."

"No," Kirk said, glaring at KerDaq. "It is not."

He put his hand on Prescott's shoulder and was surprised to feel her flinch. Her bones were fragile and his hand heavy. He hoped he hadn't hurt her. Then she smiled at him, bravely, as if she was trying to overcome fear.

"Kirk," KerDaq said.

Kirk held up his free hand for silence. KerDaq remained quiet and for the first time Kirk was thankful for a reasonable Klingon.

Then Kirk bent toward Prescott. "I want KerDaq to hear what you have to say. Please, tell us what you said earlier, and explain how it all happened."

Prescott licked her thin lips. Her gaze darted from Kirk to the Klingon to McCoy before resting on Kirk again. She looked almost frightened, as if she were in a situation her brain couldn't completely fathom. Kirk couldn't even imagine being in her shoes.

She took a deep breath, then glanced around at Folle, who nodded. When she turned back to Kirk, she seemed stronger and there was a light in her eyes.

"We had hoped to supply all our people with unlimited power," she said. "Our experiment was based on the largest moon of the ninth planet. It was the first to break up."

"This means nothing," KerDaq said, almost spitting on the floor in disgust.

"You are on my ship, KerDaq. You will listen to Prescott."

KerDaq crossed his meaty arms over his chest, but he said nothing more.

Spock, however, hadn't taken his gaze off Prescott. He stood slowly and approached her, as if she had said something that resonated for him. "What type of energy experiments were you conducting?"

A slight tremble ran through Prescott. Kirk could feel it underneath his palm. Spock made her uncomfortable, but she gave no outward sign of it. Instead she met his gaze like an equal. "We created a fusion reaction in the center of the moon, contained by a magnetic shield and the moon's natural crust."

Spock glanced at Kirk and then back at Prescott. Kirk knew exactly what he was thinking. Such an idea had been tried successfully in hundreds of systems throughout known space. It would not have had the power to break apart the moon, let alone the entire system.

KerDaq snorted in disgust and then said, "We tried such things a thousand years ago and we did not destroy our system."

"Yes," Spock said, ignoring KerDaq. "Fusion power is a tried and reliable power source for many pre-warp cultures."

"Pre-warp?" Prescott's friend, Folle, asked.

"It's a term for cultures at your level of advancement," McCoy said. Then he raised his head slightly, giving the Klingon a sideways glance, of a kind that always made Kirk wary. "So you think, Prescott, that your experiments had something to do with this destruction."

She shook her head. "I don't think it, Dr. Leonard McCoy. I know it."

"A runaway fusion reaction could not cause this kind of destruction." KerDaq said. "Any child knows that is not possible."

"Let her finish, KerDaq," Kirk snapped.

Prescott moved out from under Kirk's hand. She moved into the center of the upper deck, as far from the others as she could get. It was as if this subject was so painful, she could not take in anyone else's presence, anyone else's warmth.

Kirk let her move away. "Prescott," he said softly, carefully, unwilling to let the moment pass. "A runaway fusion reaction might have destroyed the moon, but nothing more. There was no method that could have spread a fusion reaction through space."

Prescott wrapped her arms around herself as if she didn't hear him. Folle walked up behind her. She stepped away from him. "Prescott," he said, "we didn't do it. Just like I told you."

She shook her head.

Spock's attention hadn't wavered from her. "The destruction *is,* however, centered on the location of the ninth planet. We rescued you from a base inside the moon of the fifth planet. What were you doing there?"

"Our base was the control central," Prescott said. "The first energy was to be projected to our moon. From there it would have been distributed throughout the system."

"Projected?" Kirk repeated. Suddenly he knew what had happened. He glanced at Spock, who looked almost visibly shaken. Spock knew too.

KerDaq took a step toward Prescott. "You *projected* it?" Even KerDaq had guessed what was coming next.

Kirk put up a hand for KerDaq to stop and he did.

Prescott held her ground, even though her eyes looked like those of a stunned deer. Color rose in her cheeks. Folle stood behind her like a pillar, giving her support.

Kirk swallowed. "What method," he asked slowly, "were you planning to use to project the energy?"

Prescott turned to Folle, who stepped forward. Kirk knew instantly that it had been Prescott who was behind the fusion power idea. But it was Folle who championed the method of transportation to get the energy to the inner planets.

"A form of microwave transmission," he said. He held his head high and there was no evidence of shame in his posture. He still didn't understand what had gone wrong. Nor did he accept the blame.

What had he said a moment ago? *Prescott, we didn't do it. Just like I told you.*

Just like I told you.

She had known all along and believed she had caused the death of all her people.

Kirk felt a wave of compassion run through him, despite all the destruction. She had lived for weeks with the knowledge that she had destroyed her people, and everyone around her had denied it. Denied it all.

"Microwave transmissions cannot carry or contain the power you would have received from such a fusion reaction," Spock said. "How did you solve the problem of containment?"

Folle frowned as if something in the tone of Spock's question bothered him. "We created a feedback loop, using part of the power of the beam itself to contain it."

KerDaq spit out, "Fools!"

Two dots of color appeared on Folle's cheek, but if Kirk were to wager on the cause, he would guess that Folle was angry at the accusation, not at feeling as if he were the cause.

But Prescott's gaze met Kirk's. "I know something went wrong. What was it?"

"Spock," Kirk said, indicating that he should explain.

"Your idea for energy was sound, but your delivery system was flawed," Spock said. "A microwave carrier beam is not a container. It is a strainer filled with water. Instead of carrying the water from one place to another, it runs out through the thousand holes that compose the strainer. Or in your case, your beam dripped power. It lost more power than it carried."

Folle's frown deepened. But Prescott looked vaguely relieved, as if knowing what had gone wrong helped her somehow.

"And that caused the destruction?" she asked.

"By creating a feedback wave from the lost power, you created a loop within the containment field." Spock was still explaining. He seemed to believe she needed the in-depth understanding as well as the short answers. "The loop became far more powerful than the energy it contained."

"We knew that would happen," Folle said. "We had a method of draining the containment field at the receiving end."

KerDaq snorted. "Such stupidity should be rewarded with death."

"It has been," McCoy said softly.

Kirk shivered.

And for a moment the bridge was deadly silent.

Kirk was getting a clear picture of the problem. It was nice to know the cause, but that wasn't enough. The magnitude of the destruction terrified him, and he still didn't understand why it was increasing.

Spock ignored KerDaq and McCoy and went on. "The containment field would never reach the destination. It would instantaneously feed back down into the power source itself the moment the beam was turned on."

"Setting up a feedback loop inside a fusion reaction," Kirk said.

"In essence," Spock said, "melting a hole through known space and into subspace."

"A hole that sends out destructive waves of subspace interference," KerDaq said. "Waves that destroyed my ship."

"A hole," Kirk said, "that we somehow have to close."

Chapter Seventeen

THE EMERGENCY BACKUP SYSTEMS had kicked in.

Captain Bogle liked the darkness. It reinforced the sense of urgency, and his crew always worked well when things were tough. He had diverted the main power to the shields in the last skirmish with the Klingons, but even that was failing.

The red-alert lights were blinking in the background, bathing the bridge in rotating red. The eerie color made his officers look as if they were bleeding, something that no one seemed to notice but him.

Bogle would have disconnected the red-alert lights if he could have.

But he couldn't. It seemed they were as essential to a starship as air.

On the screen before him the remaining operational Klingon ship hung silent and deadly, its green looking sick and pale against the livid red of the bridge.

"Our shields are at forty percent," Science Officer Lee said. "Not enough to withstand the coming subspace wave."

Bogle clenched his fists. The Klingons had targeted his shields. They had recognized that weakness and had gone for it. If he couldn't get more power to the shields, the Klingons would succeed in destroying the *Farragut*.

"How long do we have?" Bogle demanded.

"Two minutes," Lee said.

Bogle punched his intercom button to get his chief of engineering. "Projeff, we need more power to the shields."

"I've already diverted everything I can think of." Bogle could tell from Pro's voice that he knew the importance of the problem.

"Well, divert everything else. Including the damn red-alert lights."

"Aye, sir." Bogle thought he heard a chuckle in Projeff's voice. Pro knew how much Bogle hated those lights.

"Good," Bogle said. "Bogle out."

Four members of his bridge crew were attempting to divert power as well. Those shields were crucial, especially since the wave strength was increasing for reasons none of them could yet figure out.

And, beneath it all, he was worried that the Klingons would attack again just as the wave hit, when the *Farragut* would be at her most vulnerable.

Bogle swiveled his chair.

Lee was hunched over his science console, monitoring everything. He didn't know what he'd do without Lee.

"What's the status of the *Enterprise?*" Bogle asked.

"They seem to have taken very little damage," Lee said, shaking his head in disbelief.

Bogle shook his head, too. He didn't know how Kirk managed it. If Bogle were to lay odds, he would guess that Kirk would be the only officer in the fleet to retire without losing a ship. If he didn't get tossed out first for breaking rules.

The red-alert lights shut off, leaving the bridge in near darkness. Bogle blinked, grinning to himself. *Nice going, Projeff.*

"Sir," Gustavus said, "the *Enterprise* is hailing us."

"And sir," Lee said, "that Klingon ship off our bow is powering up."

"Wonderful," Bogle said. Just as he had predicted. The Klingons would attack when the wave hit. He hoped Pro repaired those shields in time. "Put the *Enterprise* on screen."

The screen flickered and then an image filled it. Bogle resisted the urge to rub his eyes. The Klingon commander stood beside Kirk, looking as at ease on the bridge of the *Enterprise* as her own captain did. A tiny woman stood beside them. The men dwarfed her and yet she seemed to belong in their company.

"Captain," Kirk said, a slight smile crossing his face. He knew what impact he was having and it was clear he was enjoying it. "I'd like to introduce you to Commander KerDaq." Kirk indicated the Klingon standing beside him on-screen.

KerDaq nodded, but said nothing.

Kirk's smile disappeared. Bogle saw the determination in Kirk's eyes. Even though Kirk gave the appearance of enjoying things, he knew how serious the situation was.

For all of them.

"I understand you're having shield problems," Kirk said. "Mister Spock is sending a heading and timing so that you will be able to run with the coming subspace wave to reduce its impact."

"Understood," Bogle said.

"As do I," KerDaq said. "Now I must warn my ships."

Kirk nodded. "Kirk out."

The screen went dark and then came back with the picture of the Klingon battle cruiser off their bow.

Bogle sat staring, not totally understanding what he'd just seen. Kirk and the Klingons working together. And behind them a woman had been standing silently.

An alien woman.

An obvious Tauteean survivor.

"I have the heading and coordinates," Lee said. "We have fifty seconds."

"Transfer them to navigation and be ready to initiate on the correct timing." Bogle turned to Lee. "Mister, I want a double check on those calculations within twenty seconds or we're going to jump to warp to outrun the subspace wave. I won't take any chances with this crew and this ship."

"Working, sir," Lee said.

Fifty seconds to repair the shields and to hold on. Bogle let out his breath. At least the Klingon attack he had been expecting probably wouldn't come. Not if KerDaq was on the bridge of the *Enterprise.*

"They are correct, sir," Lee said, and he actually sounded confident. Bogle couldn't see his face in the dimness, and didn't know if Lee's tone was a sign of true confidence or not.

"Explain," Bogle said.

"If we follow the course and speed given to us by the *Enterprise,* the impact of the subspace wave will be reduced by almost sixty percent. With our shields at sixty percent, we will sustain no damage."

"Understood," Bogle said. "Stand by."

."Captain," Rodriguez said. "Our shields are now at seventy percent."

Bogle grinned to himself in the darkness of the bridge. He knew those red-alert lights were wasted energy. "Good work, Pro," he muttered.

"Follow the *Enterprise* instructions, Mister Lee."

"Yes, sir," Lee said. "Mister Rodriguez, I want you to go to one-fifth impulse on my mark."

On the screen the Klingon ship was turning and aiming itself in the same direction they were heading. Bogle shook his head. How Kirk did it, Bogle would never know.

"Now, Rodriguez!" Lee said. "Impact in five seconds."

Bogle held on as his starship surfed a destructive wave.

Off the port side of the *Farragut* a Klingon battle cruiser did the same thing.

Chapter Eighteen

McCoy was starting to measure time with the *Enterprise*'s collisions with the shock waves.

After Prescott made her revelation, he had left the bridge. He had arrived in sickbay when the next shock wave hit. Then a complement of crew members arrived, sporting minor bruises. He had Nurse Chapel tend to them while he mended the broken Tauteean bones, and cleaned the gangrenous wounds.

Then the next shock wave hit. He didn't really notice it, only its effects. He treated all the minor bruises and had time to help the Klingon doctor treat a seriously injured Klingon who had been burned in the fight.

The only benefit he could see to the waves was that the influx of battered crew members always brought new information: *The* Farragut *and the Klingon vessels made it through the waves; Captain Kirk and the Klingon were working side by side; Mr. Spock, in what seemed like exasperation, asked that the* Farragut*'s science officer join them in an attempt to close the rift.*

The ensign who had imparted the last bit of information had seemed surprised that Spock would be exasperated. McCoy, on the other hand, felt no such surprise. He had known Spock for years, and it had always seemed as if their relationship had been based on exasperation—on both sides.

The waves continued, but the crew was finally catching on. During the last wave, only a few bruises had arrived. Nurse Chapel could handle them. McCoy wanted to be on the bridge. He told himself he wanted to contribute to the discussions, to see if he could provide some solution to closing the rift. But the truth was that he wanted to see Prescott.

He arrived to find the bridge crowded.

Kirk, Scotty, and KerDaq circled the science station behind Spock.

Uhura was monitoring communications, Sulu and Chekov were conferring on ways to better "surf" the wave, but Prescott was nowhere to be seen.

McCoy walked closer to the cluster of people around the science station. Prescott was seated beside Spock, her tiny hands stretched over the console. Another science officer, recognizable by his blue uniform, sat on Spock's other side. Apparently the *Farragut*'s science officer—Lee, if McCoy remembered his name correctly—was a big red-headed man who had a joviality that made Spock seem positively morose.

It was very clear to McCoy that they had made no headway at all.

McCoy stopped beside Kirk. The captain moved aside for him, and McCoy stared down at the computer screens, the scope, and the buttons that marked the tools of Spock's trade. Prescott glanced over her shoulder at him and smiled. It was an absent smile—her mind was clearly elsewhere—but it warmed him all the same.

Spock looked up from his scope. "The subspace waves are gaining in intensity, and the rift is widening."

"How long do we have?" Kirk asked.

"Not long," Lee said. His voice was deep. McCoy glanced at him in surprise. Spock would never have been satisfied with such a vague answer.

"I agree," Spock said. And then he gave the correction McCoy had been expecting. "If we do not find a solution within two hours and ten minutes, no starship will be able to approach the rift. We will be unable to close it."

Prescott leaned back. McCoy could feel the warmth of her skin against his leg. "I don't understand. There has to be a source for all this power causing the waves. Can't we just shut down the source? Maybe destroy it?"

KerDaq snorted and rolled his eyes. McCoy never realized that the Klingons could be so expressive without saying a single word.

Rather like human teenagers.

Science Officer Lee shook his head as if he couldn't believe her stupidity. Spock ignored her.

But Scotty looked at her with compassion.

"There is a source, lass," he said. "The universe is like a person's body. A person—" He glanced at KerDaq. "—well, a human at any rate, has a heart that is the main source of power within the body. The universe has a heart, for lack of a better word, an energy source that keeps the universe running. Your fusion reaction tapped that source of universal power. The problem you gave us, though, is that there is now a hole between universes, allowing the power of Universe A to spill over into Universe B at an ever-increasing rate. We just happen to be in Universe B."

The analogy wasn't as precise as Scotty had thought it was, but it still set mental bells ringing for McCoy. He had never pictured the universe like a being, with a heart and lungs, and all. If he tried to stretch the analogy, it failed. But when he first pictured it, he got an image.

And an idea.

"Jim," McCoy said, stepping forward. "What Scotty is saying, if I hear this right, is that this hole in space is very much like a bleeding cut on a human?"

"The analogy is, in fact, faulty," Spock said, "because a human does not bleed into another—"

"Give him a minute, Spock," Kirk said. "You have an idea, Bones?"

McCoy nodded. He could feel the excitement of a new—correct—discovery welling within him.

"When a patient has a cut, you don't close the entire thing at once. You work from the sides, stopping the expansion and closing it slowly."

Spock tilted his head, and gazed at a spot between all of them. McCoy knew that look. Spock was deep in thought.

"You close it from the ends," Scotty said.

"Not from the middle," Lee said almost simultaneously.

"We could be—"

"—farther away—"

"—and still close—"

"Gentlemen?" Kirk said, obviously hoping to stop the cacophony. The two men were clearly speaking the same language, but no one else could understand the subtext. They had an idea and it seemed to match.

"Captain," Scotty said, his dark eyes alight with the beauty of his idea. "If we can get close enough we could expand our warp shields out over a corner of the rip."

"The *Farragut* could do the same," Lee said, "on the other side, at the same time."

Spock tilted his head the other way, as if he were picturing it all. Then his gaze met Kirk's. "That would effectively let the covered area seal itself," Spock said.

"And both ships would implode," KerDaq said, from behind them, making McCoy jump. "I will not participate in such a foolhardy mission with Klingon ships."

Scotty leaned forward, put his hand on the console, and touched the two-dimensional image of the rift that Spock had called up earlier. "We could easily work toward the center of the rift, closing and—"

"I have to concur with Commander KerDaq," Spock said. "The moment the warp signatures expanded to cover the tear in the universe, both ships would be destroyed. We would, in essence, be creating a feedback loop similar to the original."

"At least the Vulcan has some sense," KerDaq said.

But the others ignored him. Prescott studied the diagram of the rift as if it could expand her scientific knowledge overnight. Lee and Scotty looked at each other, their minds obviously whirling. Then Scotty grabbed a chair and slid it beside the engineering console.

"There has to be a way," he said.

"The doctor might have had the right metaphor," Spock said. "But this is a wound caused by a burning hole in space. It would seem to me that instead of stitching the wound closed, we would need to cauterize it."

"You don't cauterize burns, Spock," McCoy said.

"We are speaking in metaphors, Doctor," Spock said. "We would be closing the wound in the same manner in which it was created."

McCoy was about to protest when he noticed the others around him. Lee and Scotty were frowning, deep in thought. KerDaq no longer looked so disgruntled either.

"It might work," Lee said, softly.

"Aye, lad," Scotty said. "It just might."

McCoy shook his head. It was as if both men were reading each other's mind.

"Would someone please explain the idea to me?" Kirk said, moving around the rail and back down near his chair.

"Captain," Spock said, "if we, along with the *Farragut* and two of the Klingon vessels, were to fire full phasers at the rift as a wave began, we would set up a feedback loop between the wave and the ships."

"Increasing the power of the wave," Scotty said.

"And turning the wave back on itself," Lee finished.

Spock nodded. "Effectively closing the rift in space."

"Effectively, Mister Spock?" Kirk asked.

"I don't think it matters how we do it, Jim," McCoy said, not sure if he understood the concept either, "just that the rift gets closed."

"My ships will help with such a solution," Ker-Daq said, his voice full and firm, as if the decision was now made.

McCoy glanced at the Klingon. His arms were still crossed over his chest, but he looked less threatening suddenly, as if the solution had calmed something within him.

"Captain," Spock said, swiveling on his chair, and nearly knocking Prescott aside. McCoy put a hand on her back to steady her. "There is a problem."

"Of course," Kirk said, taking a deep breath. "Isn't there always?"

McCoy almost laughed. Kirk was right. Solutions never seemed to come easy with this crew. If the time wasn't short, then the solution was impossible. He couldn't begin to remember how many times this crew had made the impossible happen.

Spock continued as if Kirk hadn't even spoken. "The resulting closure of the rift will be sudden. It will send out a final subspace wave of approximately two hundred times the destructive power we are currently experiencing."

"That's not a problem, Mister Spock," Scotty said. "The ships can simply jump to warp ahead of the wave."

Spock nodded. "Agreed, Mister Scott. The ships can jump to safety." Spock folded his hands together. McCoy noticed that Spock always made that gesture when he was about to impart bad news. "The problem I was referring to has nothing to do with the starships. The resulting wave would pulverize the rest of the large asteroids in this system. There is a sixteen percent chance the wave would collapse the Tauteean sun."

Suddenly McCoy understood Spock's point. His stomach clamped tightly, almost painfully. He could tell that Prescott didn't yet understand. She was staring at Spock.

Kirk's face went white and he dropped down into his chair. KerDaq frowned. Science Officer Lee glanced at Spock.

"I don't see the problem," Lee said. "Will the wave be powerful enough to destroy a neighboring system? By my calculations, even a wave of that intensity wouldn't have a destructive power beyond three light-years. And there are no systems within that radius."

Spock shook his head. "That is correct. Three point one light-years. Neighboring systems will feel it, but it would not be strong enough to cause damage at their distances."

Kirk sat staring ahead. McCoy knew he had no choice, and he obviously knew it. Unless they could come up with one more creative solution. The probability of that, McCoy knew, was next to nothing.

"Spock," McCoy asked, knowing the kind of chain reaction he was going to cause in Prescott, but knowing he had no way to stop it. He kept his hand on her back, supporting her. Her body was like a high-tension wire. Her subconscious knew what this was about, even if her conscious brain didn't. "How many Tauteean survivors did you estimate to remain in those asteroids?"

"Thousands, Doctor."

"More survivors?" Prescott moved so fast that her chair nearly fell over. McCoy caught it. She was in the center of the bridge in a heartbeat, confronting Kirk. "There are more survivors?"

Kirk only nodded.

"They'll be killed."

"Yes, they will," Spock said. He was watching her closely. McCoy took a step toward her, then stopped. He could do nothing more. He had to acknowledge the survivors, had to get the others searching for a solution, but that was all he could do.

"Your people created this problem. Such stupidity deserves death," KerDaq said.

Prescott spun and advanced on the Klingon. She was half his height and one-quarter his weight, but something in her eyes made the Klingon lean backward.

McCoy stepped into her path and she stopped. He was glad she did. He didn't doubt she was much more powerful than she looked. She shot a glare at the Klingon, then returned her attention to Kirk.

"Captain," Prescott said. "You can't kill the rest of my people."

"If he doesn't, lass," Scotty said, "hundreds of billions more will die."

McCoy stared at Captain Kirk, who sat staring at the main screen, not saying a word, faced with a decision that wasn't really a decision.

Faced with the fact that he would have to order the last few thousand survivors of a race to their death.

Chapter Nineteen

KIRK TURNED HIS BACK on his officers and stared at the screen before him. The rings were still expanding, gray and gold and white against the darkness of space. Sometimes beauty and destruction went hand in hand. That's what made destruction so seductive, because it could be beautiful.

Thousands and thousands of possible survivors. Even if he had a full day, he couldn't rescue them all. This was like those games that philosophers played—if you had to lose a friend to save a thousand unknown people, would you save the friend? Or let him die? Those philosophers never realized that people—real people—had to make these decisions all the time.

He had already made this decision once, and it still haunted him. He always dreamed about Edith

Keeler's face. In his dreams, he heard that scream cut off, followed by the thud. He felt the warmth of Bones in his arms, and saw the muddy brown building behind them, smelled the chemical stink of combustion engines in the air.

Let me go, Jim.

I could have saved her.

For the want of a nail, a shoe was lost. For the want of a shoe, a horse was lost. For the . . .

He shook himself, realizing that only seconds had gone by when it felt like lifetimes.

A thousand lifetimes.

If he could go back and tell the boy from Iowa that leadership meant sending people to their deaths, if he could prevent that boy from succeeding at the Academy, from rising in the ranks—

He still wouldn't do it. Even though he had inadvertently sent several people to their deaths over the years as part of his role as captain, he would go through it all again.

Even Edith.

Especially Edith.

Because someone else might have made the other choice.

The wrong choice.

She would have understood the need to block Hitler, to let Kirk's history come to pass instead of hers. She had been ahead of her time, Edith had, and that had been her doom.

All the kindness, all the good intentions in the world, couldn't change that.

She would understand this decision too, but she would rail against it. She would ask if there was some other way. And if there wasn't, she would say that even making a small difference was better than making no difference at all.

The bridge around him had grown deathly quiet. He turned around and stared at Spock. "How much time do we have?"

"We must close the rift within the next one hundred twenty-one minutes," Spock said.

A small difference . . .

Kirk felt as if the decision were being made for him. He turned to the *Farragut* science officer, Richard Lee. "Have you informed Captain Bogle?"

. . . was better . . .

Lee nodded. "Yes, sir. He is waiting for your decision."

Kirk felt a surprised chuckle escape his lips. Smart man, that Bogle. Since the solution had been worked out on the *Enterprise* bridge, Bogle was not going to second-guess Kirk. But that left the decision about the survivors on Kirk's shoulders. And Bogle would take no responsibility.

. . . than no difference at all.

And there really wasn't a decision to make. But there had to be another way.

"Spock," he said, "can we slow down the growth of the rift long enough to get more ships here?"

"Negative, Captain."

"How about getting us a few more hours, long enough to rescue as many survivors as we can fit on both ships?"

"Captain," Spock said, using that tone. Kirk hated that tone. The tone that implied he didn't get it.

The problem was, he didn't. Not really. Why did the universe keep giving him these impossible choices?

"If we fire randomly into the rift," Spock was saying, "we would make matters worse. Instead of creating our own feedback loop, we would augment the existing loop and increase the size of the subspace waves. The only way we can close the rift is to fire an exactly timed burst of energy at the moment a wave emerges. We will still get one more wave, the destructive wave we've been discussing."

No choice. He had no choice at all.

Prescott pushed her way past Bones. Her tiny features contained a mountain of emotion. She made the Klingon look tame. "Captain, you can't let the rest of my people die."

He opened his mouth, closed it again. She didn't understand. It was too theoretical for her. She didn't know that other peoples existed in the universe until a few hours ago. She couldn't make the leap—no one could make the leap—from the thousand people she knew to the billions she didn't.

He knew that from vast, painful personal experience.

"I have to," he said, even though he knew convincing her was impossible. Her face would haunt him, her pleading, along with Edith's scream.

A small difference . . .

The idea he had been groping for hit him.

He leapt out of his chair, and moved quickly to

the rail, energized again. "But with your help we can save a large number of your people."

"You're crazy, Kirk," KerDaq said.

"How?" McCoy asked, his face lighting up.

Kirk turned to Spock. "We have two hours? Correct?"

"One hour and fifty-eight minutes," Spock said.

Kirk nodded, not caring about the missing two minutes. "With your help, Prescott, and with the help of the rest of your people on board, we should be able to pinpoint the most likely places for survivors. Moon bases, sealed bases, spaceports. We have two ships. We can cram a large number of people in here if we have to." He smiled at Prescott. "At least enough to give your race a fighting chance to start over in another system."

Prescott's mouth opened. For a moment, he didn't think she would accept the proposal. Then she staggered slightly forward as stunned by his words. "A chance is all we need, Captain."

"We have three ships," KerDaq said. "And a fourth will be operational within the hour."

Kirk felt his own eyebrows rise. He couldn't trust this, any more than KerDaq could trust him. Kirk moved over and stopped in front of the Klingon. Kirk said nothing, just stared at him.

After a moment KerDaq laughed. "We have to watch you," he said. "In case you pick up your superweapon. If we happen to pick up a few survivors in the process, so much the better."

Kirk laughed with him. "It seems Starfleet will allow us to help survivors destroyed by *your* superweapon."

KerDaq nodded, still half laughing. Then his eyes froze on Kirk. "No tricks, Kirk."

"No tricks. Have my science officer explain how to surf those subspace waves to reduce damage to your ships. We can't have one of your ships being destroyed by an asteroid. We need all four ships to close the rift."

KerDaq grunted. "We need no explanation. You just be sure to survive."

"Deal," Kirk said.

Kirk turned to Prescott as KerDaq headed for the lift with Science Officer Lee. "We need locations fast."

Prescott, her eyes alive, her face beaming, jumped to Spock's side and began giving him directions.

Chapter Twenty

THE BRIDGE OF THE *Farragut* was still dark. Projeff hadn't gotten all the systems back on line. But the shields were operating at ninety percent of maximum capacity.

For what good that would do them.

Bogle sat in his command chair, his fingers tapping on the arm, thinking back to the days when both he and Kirk had served on this very ship. Somehow, mostly due to Kirk's brashness and ability to bend rules without breaking them all the way, he had been promoted. Bogle didn't totally understand how or why it had worked that way, but it had.

In those early days on the *Farragut,* they really hadn't been that close of friends. They'd played poker a lot together, but not much else. As officers they had come aboard at the same time, starting their careers as equals. But it hadn't remained that way. It had bothered Bogle for years that Kirk had been promoted to captain ahead of him. In fact, Kirk had become the youngest Starfleet officer ever to be promoted to that rank. And no matter how much Bogle tried to put that fact away, he had always held that against Kirk.

And he most likely always would.

Now, here he was, captain of the *Farragut,* Kirk's old ship. And what was he doing? He was letting decisions be made by Kirk, of all people.

Sitting here, now, Bogle felt that by deferring to Kirk regarding what to do with the Tauteeans he was putting himself and his career at a personal risk.

Kirk wasn't going to set back Bogle's career. He would make sure of that.

His science officer, Richard Lee, hadn't been back two minutes before Bogle realized what Kirk had set them all up for.

"We're supposed to do *what?*" Bogle asked.

Lee was standing beside him, a flush on his light skin. He obviously had agreed with the decision and he had known what his captain's reaction would be. The other members of the bridge crew watched in wonder.

"We're going to rescue as many survivors as possible in the next one hour and forty-eight minutes," Lee repeated. "Then we close the rift and get out of here."

Bogle closed his eyes and leaned his head back. The edge of the seat felt hard. He had just had his chair recushioned and it still felt hard. "Has Kirk ever heard of the Prime Directive?"

"It came under consideration," Lee said cautiously.

"That's good to hear," Bogle said, unable to keep the sarcasm out of his voice. He should have expected this. That was what kept running through his mind. He should have expected Kirk to throw all the rules out the window.

The thing of it was, Bogle's heart agreed with him. It was Bogle's mind—and his dedication to Starfleet—that was having the trouble. The Prime Directive should be the most important rule the Federation had. It should be much, much stronger than Kirk and the others treated it. But at the moment that was only his opinion. Starfleet seemed to take a much more relaxed attitude toward it.

"Get me Kirk," Bogle said. He gave Lee a hard stare and then turned his back on his science officer.

"Aye, sir," Gustavson replied quickly. Then after just a moment she said, "On screen, sir."

Bogle stood and stepped toward the screen as the flushed face of Kirk appeared. Before Kirk could even say a word, Bogle said, "The Prime Directive won't let you do this, Captain."

Kirk had started to smile and suddenly the smile was gone. "What are you saying, Kelly?"

Kirk was trying to pull friendship now and all that did was make Bogle even angrier. This wasn't a matter for friendship, as if they were ever friends.

Kirk might treat his crew like a bunch of friends, but Bogle believed in maintaining discipline and following the rules. And right now one of those rules was being broken—in his opinion.

"Captain," Bogle said, forcing his voice to remain clear and level. "It is clearly against the intent of the Prime Directive to rescue any more of these survivors."

Kirk took a deep breath and squared his shoulders. "They sent out a distress signal. We responded and will continue to respond."

"And so you intend to use that to get around the Prime Directive?"

Kirk frowned at Bogle. "I plan on using whatever means I can to rescue as many lives as I can."

Bogle stared at Kirk. Until that moment he hadn't realized just how much he hated Kirk for moving ahead of him so fast. But he couldn't let the hate get in the way of doing his job. And Kirk did have a point. The Tauteeans had sent out a distress call. It was a clear way of getting around the Prime Directive, at least the way it was being interpreted at the moment by Starfleet and James Kirk.

But he couldn't let his opinion of how the Prime Directive should be followed go so easily. Inside he knew he would help with the rescue, but he also knew it was against the true focus of the Prime Directive.

"You may be court-martialed," Bogle said. "Didn't you hear a word I said? This is against the intent of our number-one rule. Neither one of our ships should rescue any more survivors. They destroyed themselves and that is the natural way of things for some races."

Kirk snorted and his face got red. He stepped closer to the screen. "Listen to me, Captain Bogle. I may very well be court-martialed. But I have over an hour to rescue survivors and I'm going to pull every one I can out of those rocks. If I pay the price, fine. At least I'll be able to sleep at night."

Bogle nodded. It was time to let the argument rest—until a later time. "All right, Captain. You win . . . this time. We will do our best to help."

Kirk looked as if he was about to say something more, then realized what Bogle had said and nodded. "Good. Kirk out."

The screen went blank and then quickly came back up. The destruction of the Tauteean system spread out before Bogle. Three Klingon battle cruisers now grouped near the *Enterprise*.

Bogle turned slowly and sat down. The silence on the bridge was almost stifling. Kirk was going to go ahead and attempt a rescue and there was nothing Bogle was going to be able to do to stop him. So he might as well join him. As Kirk had said, they had asked for help. It was all the loophole he needed.

Then when they were done, they would close the rift and head for Starbase 11. And there he would begin work to make sure the letter of the Prime Directive was followed in the future.

And if Captain Kirk broke it again, he would be the youngest captain ever to lose his post.

Chapter Twenty-one

KIRK TURNED FROM the screen and clenched his fists. Bogle had always been a stickler for rules. Always.

Bogle of all people should have known that rules weren't the answer to everything. Sometimes they made the problem worse.

Like in this case.

The Prime Directive no longer applied. The culture no longer existed.

Of all the damn shortsighted egotistical times to have a philosophical discussion.

Kirk swung around and sat down. Around him the other crew members pretended that whatever was going on at their station required their full and immediate attention. Even Prescott had the common sense to remain quiet as she stood near the science station.

"Captain," Spock said, breaking into the deadly silence of the bridge as he stepped down to his accustomed place beside Kirk. "Captain Bogle is right. Our rescue mission is in direct conflict with the intent of the Prime Directive."

Kirk's fists became so tight that the skin on the back of his fingers pulled. Spock knew better. This argument was wrong.

On the main screen the scene of complete destruction spread out in front of Kirk.

"Spock," he said, pointing at the screen. "You don't really believe any Tauteeans could survive after the rift is closed."

"There is no chance, sir, that their civilization will continue here. But that has no bearing on the Prime Directive. This race caused its own destruction. The Prime Directive expressly forbids us from rescuing a race that destroys itself. The theory is that such a race could never become civilized."

"I know the theory, Spock." Kirk just didn't like it. He didn't like it at all.

"Not civilized?" Prescott asked. Her voice carried over the entire bridge. Kirk did not turn to face her. He couldn't look at her at the moment. "Who are you to judge whether or not we are civilized?"

"I was merely stating the main directive that we operate under, madam," Spock said, sounding like a polite schoolboy. "The Prime Directive forbids us from interfering with a culture that has not reached a certain level of technical sophistication.

We are even forbidden from preventing such a race from destroying itself."

"Why?" she demanded. "To keep the population down in the universe? So that you people can control more of it?"

"No," Spock said. "It is not that simple. It—"

"Every race," Kirk said, staring at the growing rings on the screen, "that has joined the Federation went through a self-destructive period. My people did so in the twentieth century, and nearly destroyed themselves hundreds of times. We survived it, on our own, and gained wisdom in doing so. Without that wisdom, we would not be here."

Staring at that—the destruction Prescott and her theories caused.

She was suddenly beside him. He could feel a stir of wind caused by her arrival. She leaned over the arm of his captain's chair, and he finally understood how she had forced a Klingon to back down. "You would let the rest of my people die and doom my race simply because of a rule?"

Kirk's mouth was dry. He couldn't answer her.

But Spock could. "The Prime Directive leaves us no choice, at least as we understand this situation at the moment."

Kirk broke his gaze away from Prescott and frowned at Spock. Even Spock disliked this. Spock was trying to give him an out, in his own Spock-like fashion.

"However, Captain," Spock said, "I would recommend that we not follow the Prime Directive."

"What?" Kirk asked, actually surprised.

Spock nodded. "In this instance, the Tauteeans

did send us a distress signal. They did ask for our help."

"I understand," Kirk said. It was technically a legal way to get those survivors. But it wasn't really enough.

"Captain, I—" Prescott snapped, but Kirk help up his hand and stopped her from saying any more. He didn't need her badgering him at this moment. He had to think. He got out of his chair and approached the screen. The debris field's slowly forming rings were stupendous in size, and in the amount of destruction it took to form them. In just over an hour and a half the *Enterprise,* the *Farragut,* and two of the Klingon ships would close the subspace rift caused by these Tauteean people. And in so closing the rift would send out one more huge, destructive wave that would completely wipe out any chance of the Tauteean people's rebuilding or rescuing themselves.

But by rescuing the Tauteean survivors, he was not only technically violating the Prime Directive, but putting every man, woman, and child in the Federation at risk. If something happened to the *Enterprise* during such a rescue operation, there wouldn't be enough firepower in the remaining ships to close the rift in time.

No matter how Kirk looked at it, Bogle was right. Rescuing more survivors was wrong. But why did he have to be the one actually killing them by closing the rift?

Then he heard himself say that out loud. "I'm killing them."

He turned around and faced Spock, who had

moved back up to the science station. "Spock, by closing the rift, we are actually killing the remaining survivors. Right?"

"That is correct, Captain," Spock said. "They would not survive such a wave."

"So follow me on this," Kirk said. "We are not allowed by regulation to kill other races. That's genocide, Spock. Earth outlawed genocide in the Geneva Conventions of the twentieth century. Genocide is something so hideous, so unthinkable that every member of the Federation outlawed it centuries ago."

He could feel the excitement starting to return. He knew he'd found the solution, the justification he could live with. He didn't know if it would hold up at a court-martial, but it would hold up in his own mind.

Spock frowned, clearly thinking. "If we do not close the rift, the Tauteean survivors will eventually die over the next five days," Spock said, "as the subspace waves increase in intensity."

"We must close the rift to save the lives of the rest of this quadrant," Kirk said. "But our actions, without a rescue operation, will kill the Tauteean race."

"That is correct, Captain," Spock said.

"Therefore *our* actions would be killing the Tauteeans, not *their* actions."

Spock raised an eyebrow and templed his fingers. "Technically we would be killing them," he said.

"It would therefore seem logical that we must rescue as many Tauteean survivors as possible," Kirk said, letting his voice rise in triumph.

"Actually, Captain, it makes no difference if our actions kill them or theirs do. The results are the same. They will die—"

"But it does make a difference, Spock." Kirk was leaning forward. He could feel the excitement course through him. This was right. He knew it. "If with their own actions, they destroy themselves, the Prime Directive applies. If our actions destroy them, we have a duty—a legal responsibility—to make certain they are provided for."

"He is right, Mister Spock," Sulu said from his console. "We have a duty."

"Technically, Mister Sulu, he is correct. But legal technicalities are often twists of a phrase, small games made to keep scholars happy. . . ."

"Am I to understand, then, Mister Spock, that you do not want to rescue the survivors?" Kirk asked.

Spock tilted his head back, then rested his folded hands across his stomach. "Captain, all life is precious."

Kirk grinned. He turned to Prescott, whose face held a mixture of anger and puzzlement. "Can you give Mister Spock possible locations of survivors?"

She almost beamed, she was smiling so hard. "I most certainly can," she said.

Kirk turned and sat down again. "Mister Sulu, lay in a course to the first location given to you by Mister Spock. We have survivors to find in a very short time."

"Yes, sir," Sulu said.

"And send Captain Bogle alternate locations," Kirk said. He'd played poker with Kelly Bogle before. He knew that underneath that rough, by-the-book exterior lay a huge heart. Captain Bogle would do his best to help, now that he had decided to go along.

Kirk dropped back into his command chair. "And Mister Spock . . . relay the outcome of the discussion we just had to Captain Bogle and Star-fleet. We may as well cover ourselves."

"Yes, sir," Spock said.

In front of him was a screen full of a destroyed system. They were going back in there to find survivors and the decision felt right.

"Ready when you are," he said.

Chapter Twenty-two

IT FELT LIKE DROWNING, only there was no water around her. Ergi lay on her back on the cool rock. The air had a thick feeling to it, stuffy. Breathing was hard. It felt better to take small breaths than large ones.

Sleeping would feel good too.

But she knew if she slept she would die.

Around her lay her family—her mother, her daughter, and her mate—as well as their friends and colleagues. Some had passed out against dark rock. Others had fallen asleep normally, their chests still rising and falling, but the breaths obviously shallow.

She sat, her arms wrapped around her knees, and watched them, guarding the only light that still worked. She wasn't sure if they would die first or if the light's reserve power would fail.

It had seemed like such a good idea a week ago. They had seen the destruction of the ninth planet. The waves rippled out from it, and she had projected, using the figures she could get from the government and her own calculations, that her planet, the sixth, would suffer the same effect.

Unless she found a way to survive.

Chunks of the ninth planet had floated off. People who were underground would survive until rescue teams found them. That's what she told her mate. He had told others, and they had crowded into the Er Mineral Mine near their home. They had stored food and other supplies, and sealed the entrance, thinking a week's worth of air would be enough.

It wasn't.

She hadn't believed, hadn't counted on the fact, that this crisis was bigger than her people. Even as her family crawled into the mine shaft, she believed that the scientists would find a way to solve the crisis.

A week, tops.

But a week hadn't been long enough. And one of the men, who had brought a portable computer with him, reported that the other planets and moons were going as well.

She knew what that meant: Even if they found a solution, it might be months, years before anyone found her.

And she simply hadn't prepared for that.

She put her hand on her daughter's head and smoothed back her hair. The girl's skin was clammy. Her lips were blue. She would be dead soon, and it was probably a merciful thing.

Then—suddenly—the entire room glowed. Ergi rubbed her eyes, but froze in midmovement.

No one had told her that when all the oxygen disappeared, she would see multicolored lights.

But she did.

What a beautiful way to die.

Tijer stood at the window, staring out into space.

He had been here for nearly a week now, his stomach twisting as he watched Space Station Alpha spin away from its own system. The planets were gone now, forming rings around the sun. The waves continued, but somehow the station held together. When he wasn't in the medical unit, he was here, in the corridor, staring out the windows at the destruction beyond.

He thought he would never feel terror again after that day the seventh planet exploded, hurling the space station out of its orbit and into deep space. He had managed to keep busy through much of it—so many injuries to attend to, so much sudden nausea—that he wasn't able to watch the spin, and he was glad of that.

By the time it ended, and he realized that he had lived, he had thought the terror would fade.

But it didn't. It existed beneath his placid surface like a tumor, growing and feeding on his system. The station's one hundred and fifty crew members were alone in space. No one would rescue them. No one could.

Isi, their botanist, believed that she would be able to grow enough food for them, using recycled wastes. Their food supplies were vast. They had just begun their mission on the station when the destruction happened.

Tijer worried about the waves. They seemed to be growing stronger, and Buk, the engineer, had mentioned that if a wave caught them wrong it would torque the entire station, shattering it in a single blow.

Instant death.

Tijer squinted at the darkness. The sun's light seemed dimmer, but something was reflecting. A new rock, hurtling toward them. Another threat. Larger rocks could shatter the protective shield.

Then he frowned. That wasn't a rock. A rock never had such a straight trajectory.

He was watching a ship.

He pressed his face against the cool triple pane. He didn't remember any ship design like that. Tauteean ships were oblong, not round. And they certainly didn't have odd tail sections.

He backed away and shook his head. He was hallucinating.

The terror had gotten too much for him.

He hurried down the corridor and reached the medical unit in time to see all his patients turn into multicolored light. He blinked, trying to clear his eyes, but his patients were fading.

He held up an arm. It wasn't solid anymore.

He was fading too.

A ship? he wondered as his body evaporated. Someone else's ship? Could the stories he'd read as a boy have been right?

Could someone else have been out there after all?

The bubble seal was cracked. Brug stood below it, wearing an oxygen mask. His companion, Docr, was putting a sealant on the bubble, but that was only temporary. A few more of those waves, and the bubble colony would collapse the way the moon had days before.

Two hundred people would die. Finally. They would die as everyone else had.

They had thought they had been lucky. They had thought that, since the moon split up and their bubble colony had survived on a tiny chunk of asteroid, their trials were over. But the trials were only beginning.

Brug hadn't counted on the waves continuing.

And getting worse.

This section of the colony was sealed off, protected since the bubble overhead was cracked. The crack would spread along the dome until it reached the inhabited areas. Then there would be nothing to hold in the atmosphere. Their oxygen helmets would only last a day or two.

"What's that?" Docr said, her voice sounding tinny in the helmet's microphone. She was pointing a gloved hand at a gray speck.

"Dirt?" Brug asked. He wasn't sure if going through all this work was worth it. Especially since they were going to die shortly anyway.

"No," she said. "It's growing."

He glanced again. He could have sworn, a moment ago, that the gray thing had been the size of a speck. Now it was the size of Docr's finger.

"I don't know," he said, suddenly interested.

"Brug," another voice said through his intercom. "You're not going to believe this."

"Try me," Brug said, squinting through the crack at the growing gray creature.

"I think a ship is heading toward this asteroid."

"I think you're wrong," Brug said. "We don't have gray ships."

"I know."

Docr looked at him. He glanced at her. Her eyes were wide. "That's impossible."

He nodded. "Mass hallucination. It was only a matter of time."

"True enough," she said, "but none of us have gone crazy yet. Control," she said to Operations, "do you have stats on that thing?"

"It's big," Control said. Brug couldn't identify the voice. "And it seems to be moving at an impossible speed. I think that—"

Control's voice stopped. It didn't get cut off, it didn't fade. It just stopped.

"Control?" Docr said. "Control? Someone? Pick up?"

There was no static on the line. The line was still open. Brug turned his dial, tried to bring in Mess, then Living. Nothing. Open lines but no voices.

"What's going on?" he asked.

"I don't know," Docr said. Then she looked up. The gray creature was over their dome, larger than the asteroid, longer than anything Brug had ever seen before.

Brug heard a faint buzzing. He turned to see Docr fade into bits of light. He faded as well, only to reappear in a room filled with tall monsters.

"I can't believe things could get worse," he said to himself, and fainted.

Chapter Twenty-three

THIS TIME, the noise was deafening. Voices talking, crying, and laughing. Some yelling in recognition. McCoy fought the urge to put his hands over his ears as he moved through the corridors.

Or over his nose. The smell was overwhelming. Nearly a thousand refugees, most of whom had not bathed since the disaster began, were shoved like cattle into the hallways, dining areas, and cargo bays of the *Enterprise.*

All the living quarters were filled, all the lounge areas, and all the maintenance closets.

McCoy got the sense of hundreds of frail filthy people with little more strength than it took to moan at him each time he touched one of them.

They were all bruised, all exhausted, and all terrified. A few seemed to think they had died and gone to the Tautee version of hell. McCoy couldn't say as he blamed them. He was beginning to wonder the same thing himself.

He had started out in sickbay, but emergency after emergency brought him deeper into the ship. He was lucky he'd been trained in field medicine or he would have been as overwhelmed as his nose and ears.

First rule of field medicine: Treat the most seriously injured.

Second rule: Don't attempt miracles.

Third rule: Attempt miracles.

And so on.

Mostly he had been working with crushed bones and collapsed lungs. These Tauteeans were so fragile, and so many of them had survived on very little oxygen. If he had had an entire field team, he would have been able to keep all the survivors alive. Now he would be lucky if he only lost a few.

McCoy found himself in the shuttle bay. The trip there had been a succession of pink and bluish blood, broken femurs and tibias, and shattered ball-and-socket joints. He only knew he was in the shuttle bay because of the shuttles parked on their spots, doors open to reveal even more Tauteeans inside.

The Tauteean he was working on was lying on one of Scotty's cabinets. It had once been spotless. Now it was covered with dirt and smudges from a hundred filthy fingers.

The Tauteean was male, young as Tauteeans went, and in a lot of pain. A gash ran across his forehead, just over his eyebrows, and when McCoy first bent over him, he had seen a bit of grayish brain matter.

A quick medical scan showed the gash to be superficial and the brain uninjured, and the man's vital signs were strong.

Rule Four: Save the minor wounds for later.

"He'll live," McCoy said to the Tauteean assistant named Nutri whom he had drafted to assist him. Nutri seemed to have some medical knowledge and had dug right in and helped. Nurse Chapel had also taken an assistant and was also checking patients. Anyone on the *Enterprise* with even a slight bit of medical knowledge had been drafted to do the same.

At least two Tauteean doctors were among the survivors. McCoy had given them a minute lesson on how to read a medical tricorder, how to close a skin wound, and how to mend a broken bone. Then he sent them deep into the bowels of the ship. He expected they'd make a number of mistakes, but it was better than nothing for most of these people.

McCoy stepped over a Tauteean with a black-and-blue eye who claimed nothing else was wrong, and bent over the next patient. This one was a young girl, who was half the size of Prescott. A child then. She was unconscious. McCoy scanned her and found that one leg had been crushed. Finesse surgery, which he just didn't have time for at the moment. He could do the major repairs now and save the minor ones for later. If he had had more time, he would have done it all at once. Instead he would have to go back in, cause her extra pain, in order to save her leg and her life.

He would be working on these people until he died.

Eighty years from now.

To make matters worse, the ship shook every five minutes. He kept losing track of the time, and so it seemed that each time he was about to do something delicate, the ship hit one of those waves.

For a while survivors poured in. As he mended that bone, and inflated this lung, he heard stories that made him marvel at the ingenuity of the Tautee people.

And made his hair curl.

He had survived some terrifying things in his day, but nothing like what these people had gone through.

Over five hundred Tauteans on the fifth planet—the original source of the Tautee people—had gone below ground into ancient bunkers built for some war fought and won centuries before. They survived on dried food stored for people long dead, and were attempting to repair the air-circulation systems when the *Enterprise* found them. A few of those survivors had lost family to botulism and other diseases McCoy had thought completely eradicated.

Fifty Tauteans on a moon of the ninth planet, near the source of the destruction, saw the readings on their computers, guessed something awful was going to happen, and took a spaceship away from the planet. They accidentally surfed the first wave, and managed to float, helpless, in space until the *Enterprise* spotted them. Many of the collapsed-lung cases came from there. McCoy also suspected he had one case of reversible brain damage from that ship.

Another hundred had holed up in a sealed laboratory on the moon of the third planet. They continued with their daily business as if nothing were wrong, and were, in McCoy's opinion, his toughest patients. They didn't want to believe he existed, didn't want his help, and wanted to return to their work. He had never seen so many cases of mass denial in his entire life.

Now the problem was where to put all the people. The cargo bays were full, the shuttle bays, including the shuttles, were jammed.

McCoy had sent the less injured, the ones who didn't need to lie down, out into the corridors to sit along the walls. But even the corridors were filling up.

"Dr. McCoy?" Captain Kirk's voice barely broke through the noise of the crowded shuttle bay.

McCoy glanced at the girl with the crushed leg. She would have to wait a moment. He moved toward the comm unit on the bulkhead, indicating that his assistant should stay beside the girl.

"Go ahead," McCoy said, tapping the intercom line open.

"Bones," Kirk said. "We are beaming another two hundred aboard."

"Damned if I know where we're going to put them," Bones said. And he didn't. There just didn't seem to be much room left.

"Doesn't matter," Kirk said. "Put them in the crew's quarters. My cabin will hold a dozen or so."

"Your cabin's full."

"It is?" Kirk seemed shocked. "Well, just find room. We're running out of time. Kirk out."

"Find room, find room, as if I'm in charge of housekeeping. What does he think I'm doing down here? Napping?" McCoy gingerly made his way back to the injured girl. His assistant was running a tricorder over her.

"She's oxygen-starved," Nutri said. "I think that's why she's unconscious."

The ship suddenly began to shake and rock, and the moans and panicked voices filling the shuttle bay increased. McCoy leaned against the bulkhead for support, and closed his eyes, not wanting to see more bones get broken, more Tauteeans get injured.

Even after an hour of these shakes, every one scared him. Every time he could imagine the *Enterprise* being tossed against a huge asteroid.

He had a vivid imagination at times. Too vivid.

When the shaking finally passed, he leaned over the girl. Nutri shook her head. "I don't think she's going to make it," Nutri said.

McCoy did a quick scan. The girl's signs were weak, but she was in no danger. And she had been without oxygen for a while, but not long enough to do any damage. She was unconscious because of the pain. And a good thing too. He wouldn't want to stay awake with that kind of injury.

McCoy made a rough splint to keep the leg straight, made certain it was clean and no bones had pierced the skin. Then he glanced at his assistant. "Find two people to carry this girl into the cargo bay. I'll fix her leg there later."

Nutri nodded and dashed off over the sprawling figures of her injured people. McCoy watched her go. He didn't know if he'd get to the girl later. He didn't know if there would be a later.

For any of them.

But he had trusted Jim Kirk before.

He had to trust him again.

Then, suddenly, his fears got worse as the lights flickered, dimmed, and then went out.

Chapter Twenty-four

AT LEAST the bridge wasn't crowded. Scotty had asked permission to beam survivors onto the bridge and Kirk had denied him. They needed open spaces here, and the ability to think without explaining each action.

Or who they were.

Or how they came to be here.

Talking to Prescott was enough.

The bridge was a place of action.

It had to remain so.

Besides, Kirk needed the space to pace. He stopped beside the science station. He didn't know how Spock could remain so calm.

And motionless.

"How much time do we have before we need to close that hole?" Kirk asked.

"Twenty-six minutes, Captain." Spock didn't even glance into his scope. Instead he kept scanning surrounding space for more survivors.

Kirk nodded and sat down in his chair. Its ruined pad felt almost welcome. He tapped his comm button. "Mister Scott. Are the last survivors out of that mine?"

They had been pulling two hundred more Tauteean survivors from a deep mine on an asteroid in the remains of the sixth planet. From Mister Spock's last count, they had rescued nine hundred and sixty Tauteeans. They had no idea how many the two Klingon ships or the *Farragut* had found.

"Aye, sir. We've got the last few and are awaiting coordinates for more," Scotty said. "Although I don't know where we'll put 'em."

More survivors. There wouldn't be any more. Even though he wanted there to be. He shook his head, marveling at the choices before him. A thousand was simply not enough.

A small difference . . .

". . . is better than no difference at all," he muttered.

"Captain?" Uhura asked. She had turned, hand to her ear, as if she had heard him in the intercom.

He shook his head again. "Just muttering, Lieutenant."

He punched the intercom button again to the transporter room. "Good work, Mister Scott. Stand by."

"Aye, sir," Scotty said.

Kirk was running out of the time or the luxury to worry about all the Tauteeans he couldn't rescue.

All he could do now, when he had quiet time—if he ever had quiet time again—was hope that Spock's estimates were wrong, that they had found every last survivor.

That *was* a possibility, wasn't it?

But he knew better than to ask.

"Captain," Spock said, glancing up from his scope. "I have found a large group of survivors in a deep, underground mining area on the fourth planet."

"How large?" Kirk wasn't really sure he wanted to know the answer.

"I would estimate there to be over eight hundred, sir."

"Eight hundred. We can't—"

Suddenly the lights flickered and then went out. In the half second of total darkness, Kirk stood. This was too much. Then the emergency lights came on-line. The display screens and the instrumentation panels provided most of the light. The crew looked ghostly, but they had all retained their positions.

"We have had a full power loss, Captain," Spock said. "All of the sensors are down."

"Communications are out," Uhura said.

"The helm is not responding," Sulu said.

Kirk glanced around, not really believing what was happening. Suddenly they were completely dead and blind in the middle of the most dangerous debris field this side of Earth. Quickly he slammed his fist onto the comm button. "Scotty! What's going on?"

There was a moment of silence; then a quavering

voice said, "Mister Scott is in the transporter room."

Kirk knew that. He had hit engineering by force of habit. He hit the comm button for the transporter room. "Mister Scott! Status!"

This time, Scotty's voice responded immediately. "Well, Captain, from what I can tell here, all this shaking and rattling around caused a short somewhere in the main circuits. The short caused a power spike large enough to knock out the main power couplings. Most of the systems are off-line."

"We noticed," Kirk said. "We can't run like this, Scotty. We need power. Now."

"I know, sir. I'll do what I can. But at the moment, I canna get you more power."

Kirk leaned toward the arm of his seat. "How long will it take to get the power back on-line?"

"I'm heading for engineering now," Scotty said. "It shouldn't be very long."

"How long, Mister Scott?"

"Ach, five minutes, maybe six," Scotty said.

"Captain," Spock said, without turning around, "the next subspace wave will hit us in exactly two minutes and eight seconds."

"Mister Scott, you have two minutes."

"Aye, sir," Scotty said.

Kirk hoped two minutes was enough time. Because if it wasn't, the *Enterprise* and the thousand Tauteean survivors on board would be smashed to a pulp against the nearest asteroid.

Chapter Twenty-five

"CAPTAIN," Science Officer Lee said, glancing up from his scope. His voice seemed to shake and his face looked pale in the blue light from his panel. "The *Enterprise* is in trouble."

"What?" Bogle jumped up from his command chair. He'd spent most of the last hour there in silence, riding out the bumps of the subspace waves, and thinking, letting his crew handle the few rescue operations. Kirk's last communiqué before the *Enterprise* went into the rings on a rescue operation had been addressed to both him and Admiral Hoffman at Starfleet. Kirk had reasoned that without the Federation and Klingons closing the rift, the Tauteean race might have a chance of survival. A small chance, but chance nonetheless. Therefore, since the Federation was causing the final destruction of the Tauteean system to save itself, a rescue operation was justified. The Prime Directive no longer applied.

Kirk had a good argument, but it was nothing more than that. Hoffman might buy it. She wasn't here. She hadn't seen the rings, or the destruction. She didn't know just how devastating it was.

But Bogle did. And he wasn't convinced. The Tauteeans would have died if the Federation didn't exist. They would have died if no one had come into their sector. They would die five days sooner because of Federation interference, but no race could save itself in only five days.

Not in circumstances like these.

Not with this kind of rift, in these kind of waves, with the Tauteeans' level of technology.

Jim Kirk knew that, and Kelly Bogle knew that.

Bogle respected Kirk enough not to argue the point at this time. But that was it. If he was called to testify, he knew what he would say.

"Sir?" Lee said.

Bogle stood and moved over to the science station. "Can you tell what's happening?" Bogle asked.

"They seem to have suddenly lost all power and engines."

Behind him Bogle heard a few gasps from his bridge crew. Without power or engines, the *Enterprise* would not survive in those waves. Damn Kirk.

Bogle turned to Gustavus. "Hail them."

"Yes, sir," she said. *"Farragut* to *Enterprise.* Come in, *Enterprise."*

Bogle waited in silence.

"Farragut to *Enterprise.* Come in, *Enterprise."*

Nothing. Bogle rubbed his thumb and forefinger together, an old nervous habit he thought he'd lost.

"Farragut to *Enterprise.* Come in, *Enterprise."*

Kirk had caused this. Kirk had gone in with no regard for Federation dictates, and now Kirk and his ship had become Bogle's responsibility.

"They may have lost communication in the power outage," Lee said. "It appears to be a shipwide failure. If that is the case, they probably also have lost sensors."

Bogle glanced at the front screen, which showed the huge debris fields slowly forming rings around the Tauteean sun. A ship stranded in there, without power, had no chance of survival.

Bogle didn't want to know the answer to the next question, but he had to ask it. "How long until the next subspace wave hits them?"

Lee studied his scope for a moment, his fingers dancing on his control board. Finally he said, "Less than two minutes, sir."

Bogle stood frozen for a moment. Not enough time to get there and help. Not enough time at all.

But he could at least try.

He turned to Rodriguez. "Take us in to the position of the *Enterprise* at the safest and fastest possible course."

After just a second, Rodriguez said, "The course is plotted."

"Do it," Bogle said. Then he turned to Lee. "Keep an eye on that wave and make sure it doesn't slam us into a damn rock."

"Understood, sir."

Bogle sat down and watched the big screen. There was little he could do now. He had to trust the skill of his navigator and his science officer. He had no other choice.

The *Farragut* and the *Enterprise* were his responsibility. He had to risk his own ship to go after James Kirk.

He hated that.

And right now he hated Jim Kirk more than anything.

Chapter Twenty-six

BLIND, DEAF, TRAPPED in a lifeless ship in the middle of a debris field. With a subspace wave on the way.

Kirk glanced at Prescott. She had gone very pale. She knew what was happening.

It had happened to her before. All of her people had been in this situation before.

He had risked his ship and his life to save as many of them as he could. He wouldn't let this stop him. He would succeed, at any cost.

"One minute until the wave hits, Captain," Spock said.

Kirk pressed the comm button so hard his finger hurt. "Mister Scott, I need power, at least to the impulse engines and the sensors."

"I'm working on it, sir," Scotty said. His voice

sounded strained and breathless, as if he'd been running.

Kirk took a deep breath and forced himself to glance around, away from the totally blank main screen. Prescott stood, her hands grasping the rail as if she'd fall off a cliff were she to let go. Kirk didn't blame her. He couldn't imagine going through what she had experienced the past few weeks.

Sulu continued to work the helm as if he could get control from his seat. Uhura was beneath the communications board, apparently trying to patch things. Chekov was beside her, offering his advice softly.

But Kirk's gaze kept coming back to the blank screen. He felt as if it were a curtain on the rest of the world, hiding but not preventing danger. Outside the thin hull of this ship, hundreds of huge rocks and asteroids floated. When the wave hit, the *Enterprise* would be in for the ride of her life.

Kirk took his finger off the comm button. "What's our status, Mister Spock?"

"We have full shields, Captain," Spock said, his face intent on the panel before him, "but no sensors or impulse power. Warp drive is still available to us, as are the docking thrusters."

"What's our chance of surviving this next wave?"

"Without impulse power and sensors," Spock said, "we have a ninety-nine-percent chance of being smashed into an asteroid too large for our shields. There is an eighty-seven-percent chance there will be no survivors from such a collision."

"Oh, no," Prescott said into the silence of the bridge. "This can't be happening."

"Sensors are back," Sulu said, his voice almost breaking in the excitement.

Kirk whirled as the main screen lit up, showing them the debris field around them.

"Thirty seconds until the wave hits," Spock said.

That last minute and a half had been the longest of Kirk's life.

"Mister Spock," Kirk asked, still staring at the screen, "can we move quickly enough with docking thrusters to avoid collisions?"

"No, sir," Spock said.

"Scotty?" Kirk said, holding his finger down on the comm button. "There's no time left. We need impulse power."

He didn't expect Scotty to answer. "Mister Spock, give Sulu the course just in case."

"I have already done so, Captain," Spock said.

Chekov made his way back down the bridge, returning to his position. Uhura had climbed back into her chair. Apparently the rewiring hadn't worked.

Kirk stepped forward and patted Sulu on the shoulder. "If we don't have impulse when the wave hits, do your best with the docking thrusters. Avoid what you can."

"Aye, sir," Sulu said.

"Ten seconds," Spock said.

Kirk retreated and sat down in his command chair.

"Nine seconds," Spock said.

His voice almost sounded calmer than the computer's.

"Eight."

Kirk grimaced. It seemed like his entire life had been lived with countdowns.

"Seven."

Maybe he did prefer the computer's voice. He was used to it counting the seconds of his life away.

"Six."

"Scotty," he said softly, not bothering to punch the comm button.

"Five."

"Hold on, everyone," Kirk said, making certain he sounded calm.

"Four."

"Captain," Scotty's voice cut through the bridge. "You got your power."

"Three."

Kirk took a deep breath. "It's all yours, Mister Sulu."

"Two."

The ship moved forward.

"One."

The moaning started and the wave hit with the force of an angry child pounding on an unwanted toy.

To Kirk this wave felt more intense than any of the others. He didn't know if it really was, or if it just seemed to be because they had come so close to dying with this one.

He managed to maintain his seat. Everyone on the bridge stayed at their stations and Prescott remained standing as the pounding shook the ship. It was amazing they hadn't had something fail before now.

Then the wave passed.

And they were still alive.

Every face on the bridge, except for Spock's, had an ear-to-ear smile. Kirk could feel himself smiling as well.

"Nice work, Mister Scott," Kirk said into the intercom.

"My poor girl will need every nut and bolt tightened after this ride," Scotty said.

"At Starbase Eleven, Mister Scott. I promise."

"I'll hold you to that, Captain."

"The *Farragut* is approaching," Chekov said.

"And they're hailing us," Uhura said.

Kirk's grin widened. He had an idea that just might work, now that Bogle had come charging to their rescue. He turned to Mister Spock. "Do we still have time to rescue those survivors you spotted?"

"Barely, sir," Spock said. "We have twenty minutes until we need to close the rift."

"That's enough time," Kirk said.

"Eight hundred people, sir," Chekov said. "They'll be hanging off the rafters."

Kirk shook his head. "No, they won't, Ensign."

"But sir, we're already filled—"

"Yes, we are, Mister Chekov. We'll need to find somewhere new to put them all." Kirk leaned back in his chair. The main screen showed the *Farragut,* a small but growing ship against the debris field.

"And I think I just might know just the place. And I'll wager they have room."

Kirk stood.

"Answer the hail, Lieutenant, and put this on screen," Kirk said. "Let's see just how good a poker player my old friend Bogle really is."

Chapter Twenty-seven

THE SHAKING FROM the last wave passed. Bogle's
crew had learned to ride the waves out. No one had
lost his seat, no one had even moved a finger except
for balance.

And no one said a word.

Bogle stared at the screen, but it didn't tell him
much. Kirk, the *Enterprise,* and even the survivors
worried him.

Even the survivors.

Bogle shook his head, and turned. Lee was
staring into his scope. His long body was tense, and
his hands were gripping the science console.

His knuckles were white.

"Mr. Lee?" Bogle asked, not really wanting the
answer. Without power, no ship would have survived that wave.

Lee stood slowly. "They made it. Looks like they got their impulse engines back on line at the last second."

Bogle let out the breath he hadn't realized he was holding. This system was disaster enough for all of them. They didn't need to lose the *Enterprise* too.

At least, not on his watch.

"Hail them," he said as he turned back to the screen.

"Aye, sir," Gustavus said. *"Farragut to Enterprise, come in, Enterprise."*

Outlined against the debris, the *Enterprise* was moving slowly toward them. She had a battered look, some of her lights were off, but she looked sleek and powerful, like the flagship she was.

After a moment, Gustavus said, "I have the *Enterprise,* sir."

"On screen," Bogle said. He moved closer. He forced himself to show his most calm face. Right now he was relieved. Underneath, though, he was furious. Kirk had put four hundred of his people in danger while he broke the Prime Directive. And then he had put Bogle's ship at risk.

The image on the screen shifted from the exterior of the *Enterprise* to the interior. Kirk smiled as the picture cleared. He looked even more beat-up and tousled than he had an hour before. Bogle imagined he didn't look much better.

"Thanks for coming to help," Kirk said. "That was a close one."

Bogle nodded. "I know. Do you still need assistance?"

Kirk glanced around and then looked back at

Bogle. "Actually, we do. My chief engineer informs me that the *Enterprise* is still having problems. He needs to shut down the environmental controls on some of the lower decks. The problem is that we are stuffed to the gills with survivors. How many have you picked up? I'd like to beam some over to you."

Bogle glanced back at Lee who answered softly, "We have found a little over three hundred."

Bogle nodded and turned back to Kirk. "We have over three hundred," Bogle said. "I doubt we could take too many more."

Kirk laughed. "We're almost at a thousand. And if the environmental controls go, then I hurt them. We might even lose some of the injured ones."

Bogle glanced at Lee. Lee shrugged and mouthed, *his controls look fine.* Kirk was bluffing. He was trying to manipulate Bogle, and the manipulation wouldn't work.

"Take the risk, Jim," Bogle said. "I get the ploy and I think we have enough for now."

The smile left Jim Kirk's face. "Kelly, I'm the one who takes the responsibility here. You're going to make certain I'm court-martialed when we get back, if my guess is correct. Take some more of the evidence with you. I'd hate to be court-martialed for saving lives I later lost."

Bogle laughed. He couldn't believe Kirk was even asking this. What was his reason? It made no sense.

"Kelly," Kirk said. "I'll go on record that you had no part in the rescue and it was my decision completely."

"I rescued survivors, also," Bogle reminded him. "I am perfectly capable of standing for my own decisions."

"Are you, Kelly?" Kirk asked. "Are you really? Or are you just using the Prime Directive as a shield to hide behind? You're afraid to take risks. Afraid to do anything that would jeopardize this marvelous career of yours. But being a starship captain is all about taking risks, Kelly, and if you don't have the guts to do so, then you'll always be one step behind the rest of us."

That stung. Bogle felt his face go red, even though he didn't want it to. Bogle hated Kirk for his fast promotions and now Kirk was tossing the fact at him like a weapon. How could Kirk have known how he felt?

Bogle forced himself to take a deep breath. "You just don't understand, do you, Jim? Rules such as the Prime Directive were made for reasons. Damn good reasons. Not just so you could go running around the sector breaking them."

"I don't run around the sector breaking them," Kirk said. "But I do know when taking a risk is important." He motioned behind him. A tiny humanoid woman climbed into view. She had a bruise on her forehead, and her wide eyes held a strain that Bogle couldn't even begin to understand. "Right now, I doubt our rules would carry much weight with Prescott and her people below."

Across the distance between the two starships, the woman held Kelly's gaze until he finally had to look away. Kirk played dirty. Putting a face instead of just a rule on these people made it harder.

"Your environmental controls aren't really going, are they, Jim?"

Kirk put a hand on Prescott's shoulder. "They're strained to the breaking point, Kelly, and anything else I might do would strain them further. Let's give these people the best chance we can. You've got the room."

The woman didn't say anything. She didn't have to. Her wide eyes said it all. Even if Kirk was lying, even if he was scheming, Bogle now had a face that would haunt his dreams.

And if something did happen to the *Enterprise*, it would be his nightmares.

He glanced at Lee. "How long would it take to beam a large number of survivors aboard?"

"With all the transporters," Lee said, "including cargo transporters of both ships, not long. Maybe five minutes."

"Four point eight minutes for six hundred," Bogle heard someone say behind Kirk.

Bogle faced Kirk. "Do it. Get them over here. Then let's go close that rift and get out of here."

Kirk broke into a smile. "We'll do it. And, Kelly, thanks."

The screen went blank.

Bogle turned to Lee and said, "Give the order to get the evacuation started and let me know the moment we have them all. I want to get out of here."

"Yes sir," Lee said and turned to his panel. Bogle couldn't tell if he was smiling or not.

"And watch out for the next wave."

"Yes sir," Lee said again.

Bogle dropped down into his command chair. Bogle had watched Kirk play poker. Kirk bluffed, a lot.

Bogle also knew that the environmental controls on the *Enterprise* weren't reason enough to ship the survivors over to the *Farragut*. No, Kirk had a plan. A clear plan which he wasn't going to share with Bogle.

There was sixteen minutes left until they had to close that rift. Sixteen long minutes. That gave Kirk a lot of extra time. The question was, what was he going to do with it?

Chapter Twenty-eight

BOGLE HAD GIVEN IN. Prescott had done it. Bogle hadn't been able to argue the rules while Prescott was staring him in the face.

Kirk should have skipped the entire business of the environmental controls. While it was true, on an odd sort of level—the *Enterprise* wouldn't have been able to support all the new survivors and the old—it hadn't been nearly as convincing as Prescott herself.

Kirk squeezed her shoulder, then spun and hit his comm button. "Scotty, we're emergency-beaming seven hundred Tauteean survivors over to the *Farragut*. Coordinate with them, and do it fast."

"But, Captain, I need to work on the *Enterprise*

herself. She's not in top shape yet and we still have some business here in this rift."

Kirk grinned. Scotty always wanted to work on his ship over everything else. "I know that, Mr. Scott. Keep it together as best you can. But unload the survivors. Fast. Kirk out."

Kirk punched the comm button again. "Dr. McCoy, to the bridge at once."

"On my way," McCoy's voice came back.

Kirk smiled at Spock. "He's not going to like this one at all."

Spock looked puzzled. "I do not understand what Dr. McCoy's enjoyment of a situation has to do with the rescue of more survivors."

Kirk laughed and waved his hand from side to side. "Never mind. Just tell me how long it will take us to get to those survivors you found, get them aboard, and get to the rift."

"The new group of survivors number, at my latest count, approximately nine hundred and eighty. They are under a very thin layer of rock, which will allow us to bring them aboard in eight point six minutes."

Kirk nodded. They could do that, if everything kept working. "Will it give us enough time to get to the rift?"

"Yes, Captain. We will have almost two minutes to spare."

"Two minutes," Kirk said. Two minutes. For the Tauteean people, those two minutes might be an entire future. "Spock, I want you to keep me informed the second we fall behind schedule. If we fall behind. Getting that rift closed is much more important than the last few hundred survivors."

He glanced at Prescott, who was frowning from his last statement. "I'm sorry, but it is."

She nodded, but the frown didn't leave her face.

Behind her, the lift doors burst open and Dr. McCoy came out, looking dirty, tired, and angry. "Jim, just what in blazes is going on? I had a roomful of Tauteean survivors beamed right out from under my nose."

"We're putting them back on the rocks," Kirk said. Then, before Dr. McCoy could have a brain hemorrhage, he laughed. "We're moving them all to the *Farragut.*"

McCoy seemed to stammer for a minute as Chekov and Sulu both chuckled at the joke. Then he said, "For heaven's sake, why?"

Kirk let himself drop down into his chair before he answered. "Because there are nine hundred more we're going to bring aboard." He swung so he could see the doctor's face. "So be ready."

McCoy opened his mouth, then closed it, then opened it again. But not one word came out. "How long?"

Kirk glanced at Spock. "The last of the survivors we have aboard are just being transported to the *Farragut.* I would say the new survivors will start arriving in about two minutes."

Kirk swung back around to face the front screen. He'd better say something to Bogle before they left. No point in having him too angry. "Give me the *Farragut.*"

After a moment Uhura said, "On screen, sir."

Kirk stood as Bogle's face came into view. "Thanks, Kelly," Kirk said.

"See you at the rift?" Bogle said.

"We're on our way," Kirk said, and then cut the screen.

Then he said to the air in front of him, "We just have a few passengers to pick up first."

Chapter Twenty-nine

THE ENVIRONMENTAL CONTROLS *were* strained. Spock's estimate had been off. Instead of nine hundred and eighty survivors on the surface below, there had been nine hundred and eighty on the first level. Another five hundred had been on the level below.

The *Enterprise* had beamed them all aboard, and Scotty said they were crammed like breeding gophers under an island green, something Kirk hadn't understood. Sulu had said Scotty was using a golf metaphor, and Kirk didn't ask any more.

He had tried golf once, in Iowa as a boy.

He preferred chess.

Or basketball. Either all cerebral activity or none.

And here he was, in the middle of a crisis, pondering a golf analogy.

"Captain"—Scotty's voice sounded harried over the comm—"I do think we should move some of these poor folks to the bridge."

"No, Mister Scott." Kirk sat on his chair, then winced and stood abruptly. The pad was completely gone now. "They stay belowdecks."

Kirk still needed the thinking room. Even if the survivors were packed below. He was glad Bogle had taken the rest. The *Enterprise* was strained almost beyond her capacity, and they weren't done yet.

"Captain," Prescott said. "Do you think we have time to find one more group?"

And one more, and one more. She would keep asking, and they would miss their opportunity. Kirk looked into her exhausted, bruised face. This was the face that even the good tightass Captain Kelly Bogle couldn't refuse.

But Kirk had to.

"We're out of time, Prescott," he said. "I'm sorry." Then he turned to Sulu. "Take us to the rendezvous point near the rift."

"Aye, sir," Sulu said. His fingers moved across the board. "Course laid in. We're on our way."

He sounded almost relieved. Maybe he was. The sooner they got to the rendezvous point, the sooner this would all be over.

He hit the comm button. "Mister Scott. Return to engineering. We'll need you there."

"Aye, sir," Scotty said. He sounded relieved too.

Kirk sat down despite the ruined pad. "Are the other ships in position?" he asked.

"The *Farragut* and the Klingon ship *QuaQa* carrying KerDaq are in position," Spock said. "The Klingon ship *SorDaq* is headed in that direction and will arrive in one minute."

"Good," Kirk said, leaning back and watching as the *Enterprise* moved above the plane of the destroyed solar system and headed for the debris field of the ninth planet. "What's our estimated arrival time, Mister Sulu?"

"We'll be there in two minutes, sir," Sulu said.

"So fast," a voice said from behind Kirk.

He swiveled his chair. Prescott was standing at the rail, her arms resting on it, staring at the screen. She was so short that she looked like a little girl peering over a fence. Her face had that look of awe and wonder that he had seen on others, and felt a few times himself.

"What took us weeks to travel you do in minutes," Prescott said. "And you travel between the stars? Not one of my people dared dream of such a thing. We always just assumed it was impossible."

"Sometimes dreaming is the only way to find ways to do the impossible," Kirk said.

Prescott pulled her gaze from the screen and met his. Here, he knew, was a woman who would continue to lead her people. She had nearly destroyed them, but she had also helped rescue them. Sometimes that culpability, that guilt, made survivors try even harder.

They all had a long road ahead of them.

"I see now that you are right, Captain. Our

problem was that we were too cautious, our dreams too small," she said.

"It seems to me," Spock said, "that the dream of unlimited energy for your people is not small."

"Yes it is," she said, "when we could have had the stars." And then she smiled.

"Captain," Spock said. "We have reached the designated point. All four ships are in place. The third Klingon ship, *Suqlaw,* is waiting outside the system."

"Understood," Kirk said. "Lieutenant Uhura, patch me in to the other three ship captains. Make sure they can also see each other."

"Yes, sir," she said. The picture of the other ships on the main screen dissolved and was replaced by a divided screen showing three faces, one human and two Klingon. Captain Bogle, a streak of dirt across his chin, nodded to Kirk.

KerDaq glowered. Kirk could see survivors behind him.

The unknown Klingon captain squinted at Kirk. Kirk squinted back.

"I am Commander Kutpon," the new Klingon said, in what was obviously the most menacing tone he could manage.

"Captain Kirk," Kirk said, deciding not to play that game. KerDaq could explain to Kutpon that relations with the Federation were cordial, for the moment. "I hope the hunting went well for everyone."

"We have gathered over two hundred survivors," Kutpon said.

"We also have two hundred crammed aboard," KerDaq said.

"The Tauteean people will hold you in great honor for your bravery," Kirk said before Bogle could say anything. There was no point in getting into a useless numbers game over who rescued the most.

Bogle clearly understood. "You crammed us full, Jim. And I see you made another stop on the way."

Kirk shrugged. "We found we had the room."

Bogle just shook his head in obvious disgust. Kirk wasn't sure if Kelly was mad at him, or himself. "And how are your environmental controls?"

"Strained to the breaking point," Kirk said, and suppressed a grin.

Bogle nodded. "I suspect you're right. If we hadn't had our rendezvous, you would have lost your environmental controls. Funny how that works, isn't it? Too many bodies in too small a space."

Kirk shrugged. "Just planning ahead, Kelly."

"Obviously," Bogle said.

"We have two minutes, Captain," Spock said.

Kirk took a deep breath and felt his grin fade. The serious work had begun. He faced the other three captains. "Are we all clear on what we're going to attempt?"

KerDaq snorted. "Of course we are, Captain. A single blast from each ship timed together will close the hole."

Kirk could see the other captains nodding in unison. It seemed that everyone had been briefed.

"Mister Spock will count down to the firing time. The moment after you have fired your full burst, jump to warp. You will have only thirty seconds to get out of the subspace wave's path.'"

All three captains nodded again.

The Klingons and the Federation might be enemies, but that didn't stop them from respecting each other. KerDaq was an excellent captain. Kirk had no doubt that Kutpon was the same. They knew the risks they would place their ships under, the possible damage that could occur.

Of course, if this didn't work, the damage wouldn't matter. This rift in space would destroy this entire sector of the galaxy and no one would live through it.

"The nearest starbase, Starbase Eleven, is only a half day away," Bogle said. "We can dock there. With the survivors." He said the last with a touch of sarcasm.

"Understood," KerDaq said. "We will be there."

His third of the screen went blank.

"And so will we," Kutpon said.

His section of the screen went dark as well.

Bogle said. "And good luck. We'll talk when we reach the starbase."

"I am looking forward to it," Kirk said. "And good luck to you, too. We're all going to need it. Kirk out."

The screen went back to showing the four ships spaced in a square formation above the debris field of the ninth planet.

"We have one minute, Captain," Spock said.

Kirk glanced around. Uhura was still monitoring

communications. Sulu was staring at the screen. Chekov was double-checking the coordinates.

Prescott leaned against the railing, her feet barely touching the ground. Her slender face was lined with tension. Spock was bent over his scope, looking as unruffled as ever. Only the ensigns sitting off to the sides seemed frightened. And even they were working.

They were the only sign that this moment was different from any other, that they faced more danger than they ever had.

Kirk's crew was the best in the galaxy.

He only hoped they would be good enough.

"Course laid in for Starbase Eleven," Sulu said.

"Lasers armed and ready, sir," Chekov said.

"Good," Kirk said. "On Mister Spock's mark."

"Thirty seconds," Spock said.

"Are all four ships' weapons powered up?" Kirk asked.

"They are, sir," Chekov said.

Thirty seconds seemed like an eternity. Kirk resisted the urge to stand and pace. He needed to focus all his concentration on that shot.

Because it was the only one they would ever have. The only one, or the last one, depending on whether they hit their target or not.

"Ten seconds," Spock said.

Kirk gripped the armrest.

"Nine."

Another countdown. Someday he would have to count down how many countdowns he'd been in.

"Eight."

He watched the other ships get into position.

"Seven."

Chekov checked the coordinates again.

"Six."

Prescott braced herself against the rail.

"Five."

Uhura swiveled so that she could see the screen.

"Four."

Kirk leaned forward, his stomach in knots.

"Three."

The ensigns stopped working and watched, their expressions guarded.

"Two."

Spock raised his head out of the scope.

"One."

Kirk clenched his fist.

"Fire!" Spock said.

On the screen Kirk could see the other three ships firing and the beam from the *Enterprise* joining theirs at a point below in the destruction.

A long red line grew wide and powerful, like a stream of water poured from a pitcher. Kirk felt that if he tilted the *Enterprise* slightly, he could see through the debris hole into the next universe.

Then, as a unit, all four beams from the ships cut off.

"We hit our target," Spock said with an amazing lack of excitement. Sometimes Kirk wondered how he managed that flat tone in life-threatening situations. "The feedback loop is building as planned."

"Get us out of here, Mister Sulu," Kirk snapped. "Warp four."

"Aye, sir," Sulu said. He ran his hand up the board as he said, "Engaging."

Nothing.

Absolutely nothing happened.

The screen remained focused on the asteroids below. None of the other three ships remained. All had jumped to warp. Kirk couldn't see the huge destructive subspace wave building up below, but he knew it was coming.

"Mister Sulu!" Kirk said.

"The warp drive is off-line!" Sulu said, his voice suddenly on the edge and rising.

Kirk punched the comm button. "Mister Scott, we lost warp."

"I know, sir," the voice came right back. "All this shaking and rattling knocked the coils out of alignment. I warned you this might happen."

"The wave will hit in twenty seconds," Spock said with annoying calm.

"Oh, no," Prescott said behind Kirk. "This can't be happening."

"Fix it, Scotty. Now!"

"I canna fix her in twenty seconds, sir," Scotty said.

"I can't hold off that wave."

"I know, sir. If we had a minute, maybe. But a minute might as well be forever."

Forever. Way too long. They had less than twenty seconds to figure out a way to survive.

Twenty very short seconds.

Chapter Thirty

LESS THAN TWENTY SECONDS.

They had to do something.

Kirk opened his eyes. All he saw was Prescott, her hands pressed to her face.

He saved her people only to lose them again.

"Scotty!" Kirk shouted into the comm line. "Get those warp drives up! And put any extra power you can to the shields. Now."

"Aye, sir," Scott said.

"The rift is closing," Spock said. "We have fifteen seconds until the subspace wave reaches this location."

Kirk couldn't believe this was happening. There had been no warning.

Of course, there might have been, but he had

assigned Scotty to the transporter room. Scotty usually always babied that warp engine. He'd have noticed if anything were going wrong.

But he hadn't been there.

Kirk had thought he needed Scotty to supervise the tricky transports.

And he had.

He needed a dozen Scotties.

Right now.

"Mister Sulu," he snapped. "Take us directly away from that rift at full impulse!"

"Aye, sir," Sulu said.

The screen showed the destroyed system angling away out of view, then a starfield.

"At this speed," Spock said, "the subspace wave will reach and overtake us in fifty-one seconds."

He had bought some time.

Scotty, do your magic.

Now.

Kirk turned to Spock. "What are the odds we can surf this one out and survive?"

Spock shook his head. "There are too many factors. I could not give you an accurate estimation."

"Guess, Spock," Kirk said, his hands doubled into fists.

Spock leaned back. "I believe there is a less than zero-point-one-percent chance shields will hold and the hull will not breach."

"Nice guess," Kirk said.

"I do my best," Spock said.

"Are we going to die?" Prescott asked.

"Not if I can help it," Kirk said. "But I'd hang on to something real tight in the meantime."

He punched the comm link. "Scotty? Warp?"

"The engine's on-line, Captain, but she's not responding."

"I thought you said we had a minute, Scotty. You should have had plenty of time."

"A minute to get her back on-line, Captain. But I didna say she was going to work."

"Well, keep trying." Kirk punched the intercom off.

Spock stood and clasped his hands behind his back, as if he were going to make an important pronouncement. "The rift has closed."

They had succeeded, but they could not celebrate. The first time, he had saved the galaxy by sacrificing Edith. This time, he was saving the galaxy by sacrificing himself and his crew.

And fourteen hundred and eighty Tauteean survivors.

He would not lose to the galaxy twice.

He.

Would.

Not.

He turned to Spock. "Is there any way to get any more impulse power?"

"No," Spock said. "Not *enough* power, anyway. But I do have an idea."

"Make it quick," Kirk said.

Spock bowed his head once. Then he stepped forward, and all the repressed emotion, the excitement and the fear, was in his eyes. But not his voice. "We must apply Dr. McCoy's theory again. We cannot defeat the entire wave. But we can modify a small section of it."

"How, Spock?"

"At the precise moment that the wave overtakes us, we use a photon-torpedo blast to cut down the intensity of that small section of the wave."

Kirk frowned. "Like cutting a hole through it for us to ride in?"

"Precisely," Spock said.

"Would ten photon torpedoes be better?"

"If they are concentrated," Spock said, "at the exact point and time that the wave would hit us."

"Spock, you're brilliant," Kirk said. He leapt out of his chair. "Chekov, arm ten photon torpedoes and wait for Mister Spock's mark."

"Armed and ready, sir," Chekov said.

Spock had returned to his chair. He was peering into the scope again, his fingers flying over the keys in front of him. "We have twenty seconds," he said.

Kirk paced the area behind the helm. Twenty seconds suddenly felt like an eternity. A moment ago they had seemed like nothing. He stopped beside his chair and punched the intercom.

"Scotty?"

"She's a stubborn wee beastie, Captain."

"I'll take that as a no." He had hoped the warp would come back, but now that it wasn't, he had to do something else.

He hit the shipwide comm button. "This is the captain speaking. Brace yourselves. This last wave will be greater than anything we've experienced.

Hold on tight and do not move until the bumping ends. Captain out."

"The wave will hit in ten seconds," Spock said.

Prescott slid under the nearest console. Uhura wrapped her boots around the base of her chair. Chekov gripped the sides of his console.

"Scotty?" Kirk said into his intercom.

"I'm sorry, sir," Scotty said, the exasperation clear in his voice. "but I canna do it. She's taken too great a beating."

"Five seconds," Spock said. His chair was all the way against the console. But he hadn't grabbed anything yet.

Neither had Kirk.

Kirk returned to his chair and gripped the arms. He would rather have joined Prescott under the console, but he had to stay here to monitor everything.

"On my mark, Mister Chekov," Spock said.

Some crewmen had also crawled under the consoles. Kirk almost reprimanded them, but then decided against it. He didn't really need them at the moment anyway. Sulu followed Uhura's example, and wrapped his legs around his chair.

"Fire!" Spock said.

The ship rocked as the photon torpedoes fired.

Then the wave hit.

It felt as if the *Enterprise* had slammed into an interstellar wall. The ship rocked forward, then stopped, before propelling backward and bouncing along the surface of something Kirk couldn't see.

The lights went off, the computer began reciting

damage statistics, and the screen went dead. Sparks flew from the consoles and someone screamed.

Kirk hung on to the chair as hard as he could, but he didn't stand much of a chance of staying in it.

Chekov flew past him, twirling in the air like a top.

The ship felt like a bucking horse. Kirk rode his chair for the first few major jolts and then it moved down when he was moving up.

He lost his grip on the arms and soared through the air, as he had done as a boy on his second riding lesson.

Time seemed to stop, yet the bridge was a blur of noise and darkness and sparks around him.

He slammed into the navigation console, and felt a pain so deep that his body couldn't encompass it all.

Something was wrong.

His mind wanted to leave.

But it couldn't.

He'd fallen before and remained conscious.

He reached for the console, in an attempt to stand up.

Then everything went black.

Chapter Thirty-one

McCoy was in the cargo bay.

The elderly man in front of him seemed to have suffered the Tauteean form of a heart attack. McCoy had somehow kept the man from dying, but he wasn't sure how long that would continue. He was still clueless about Tauteean internal physiology. He had sent for one of the Tauteean doctors, and hoped she would know what to do.

A young Tauteean woman named Dicnar was preparing the next patient, quizzing her about the various pains, seeing if the emergency could wait. She wasn't as good as Nutri had been, but she was working out just fine.

The noise and stench here was as overpowering as it had been everywhere else. Only here, the noise came from the moans of the injured, and the stench was that of damaged and rotting flesh.

Some of these wounds had suppurated for over a week. McCoy shuddered to think of it.

He had made the cargo bay an emergency facility. He hadn't been able to work in the shuttle bay, where a large number of this new group had arrived. And there was no way he could make it to sickbay. The patients in here were seriously ill, and might not even survive until the next day.

He had to tend to them first.

Back to rule number one of emergency care.

But he wasn't thinking about his patients at the moment. He was worrying. The captain's voice had just come over the intercom, telling everyone to hold on. Something had gone terribly wrong. They should have jumped to warp and been away from the subspace waves of destruction. But obviously they hadn't.

And except for his assistant, McCoy was the only mobile person in the entire bay. He couldn't secure these people. There wasn't even a place to secure himself.

Earlier, security guards had tied off the barrels that Scotty kept down here, but McCoy wasn't even certain those ties would hold. He needed a good old-fashioned forcefield, but since the lights had just flickered and dimmed down here, he doubted there was enough power for that, either.

He glanced around. He needed something to hang on to.

"The support beam, Dicnar," he said, and hurried over the supine patients to the middle of the bay. Dicnar was right behind him. They clung to the support beam like prisoners tied to a sailing mast.

Then the deck came alive under his feet.

A huge rumbling shook everything, and the deck bucked like a blanket being flapped out over a bed.

Up.

Down.

Up.

Then down hard again.

His patients flew like leaves in a violent wind-storm. Dicnar was screaming, and McCoy watched in horror as the fragile, horribly ill Tauteeans slammed into each other, into walls, and onto the floor.

He would lose them.

He would lose them all.

Then the floor bucked particularly hard, yanking him loose and tossing him into the air. He tried to regain his balance, but the effort was futile. He wrapped his arms around his head, brought his knees up to protect his chest, and watched the ground careen toward him.

He landed on top of a Tauteean who had a severed leg. McCoy could feel the man's bones breaking. Or maybe they were McCoy's bones. He didn't want to think about that.

Two more hard, sharp shakes that sent him into the air again and then the deck became a solid place again under him.

He waited for the next shock, but it didn't come.

Slowly, making sure he still had all his bones intact, he stood. He was going to be sore for days, but at least he was alive. He wagered that was a great deal more than he could say for some of his patients around him.

The man he landed on had gone white with pain. His remaining leg was twisted and flattened.

But he wasn't the only one.

What had once been neat rows of the desperately sick Tauteeans was now a jumble of flesh and bedding and clothes. He couldn't tell in many places where one patient started and another left off.

A few feet in front of him, Dicnar pulled herself to her feet and with a dazed look, glanced around.

"Dicnar," McCoy said over the slowly growing moaning sounds filling the room. "Are you all right?"

She nodded, turning to face him. She had hit her head. Above her right eye a large purple knot was welling up.

"Stay right there," he said. He quickly glanced around until he saw his medical tricorder near the pillar he had been originally holding. He grabbed the tricorder, and by stepping over a few unconscious Tauteeans, he was at Dicnar's side.

"You'll live," he said, shutting off his scanner after just a moment. "Although you may regret it when the headache hits. Think you can help me here?"

She nodded, then put her hand to the side of her face. The movement must have hurt.

McCoy had to take her mind off it, just as he had to take his mind off the throbbing in his knees.

"Good." McCoy glanced around. A few more of the Tauteeans were getting to their feet. They all glanced at him as if asking him what they should do. It was so overwhelming. He knew how bad this room looked, and this room was just one of many.

Now, instead of all the old injuries, there were a series of new ones as well.

And the lights were still dim.

The ship was in trouble, too.

The barrels had remained in place. The bodies had piled on the left side of the cargo bay, just beneath the barrels, leading McCoy to think that the ship had tilted somehow, had lost part of her internal stabilizer. The right side of the room was bare.

"Dicnar," he said, "let's start up in the right corner and straighten this mess out. Let's see what we have here."

Now.

Now that things had gotten worse.

He would be at this for days. Why didn't Starfleet listen to him? Why weren't there more medical personnel on starships? It wasn't as if a trip into space was a walk in the park.

"Dr. McCoy to the bridge," the intercom said, barely audible as the moaning in the room grew. It sounded like Sulu's voice, but he couldn't tell.

He glared at the faraway voice. He was needed here. Here, dammit.

"Go," Dicnar said. "I'll start here."

Even she understood Starfleet protocol, even though she'd only been on the ship for a few minutes. The doctor had to treat the bridge staff first. If he didn't, the ship's most important personnel might die and leave them all stranded.

"I'll be back as soon as I can," he said.

But she had already turned and bent over the survivor closest to the right corner.

He headed for the bridge, stepping over moaning people as he went.

This was impossible. If it was this bad here, no telling what the rest of the ship looked like.

And who was injured or dying on the bridge. He didn't want to think about those possibilities at all.

The door from the cargo bay opened onto a scene of total destruction. Ceiling tiles had fallen all over and the hundreds of Tauteean survivors who had littered the halls had been tossed everywhere. Many were getting back to their feet and trying to help their friends, but others weren't so lucky.

He slowly worked his way up the hall, helping those he could help quickly. Whoever was hurt on the bridge was just going to have to wait a little longer. This situation was impossible.

Just impossible.

Chapter Thirty-Two

THE *FARRAGUT* FELT like a refugee leaving the site of a thousand-year war. It wouldn't have been so bad, Bogle thought, if it weren't for that last group of survivors. Kirk had sent over more than Bogle expected, and there'd been no room for them in the lower decks.

He had to put them on the bridge.

He had forgotten how badly people smelled when they'd been locked up together in a small research station with no running water. He had surreptitiously ordered the air-filtration system on high, but it hadn't helped much.

No wonder Kirk had been concerned about his environmental systems. Even if an extra thousand people could have breathed the air, the systems wouldn't have been able to handle the stench.

Bogle gripped the arms of his command chair, alternately cursing Kirk and feeling half-relieved that he had helped the man. Not helping would have haunted Bogle's sleep for years.

The difference between him and Kirk was that Bogle followed the rules, even when they gave him nightmares.

Kirk didn't.

But in this case, Kirk had an argument that Starfleet would probably buy. And Kirk had made the decision. Bogle hadn't. But he would, in his private logs and in his off-the-record communications with the admirals, make it clear that he never wanted to work with James Kirk again.

Their styles were too different.

And the next time, Bogle might end up fighting Kirk instead of solving whatever problem was at hand.

"Captain," Richard Lee said, standing up from his scope. Bogle hated it when Lee used that tone. It meant something else had gone wrong. "The *Enterprise* didn't jump to warp."

"What?" Bogle asked. He swiveled his chair and nearly hit an elderly Tauteean woman in the head. Of all the stupid things to do. Kirk should have known better. No one could surf that wave, not even that damn James T. Kirk.

What was Kirk thinking?

Bogle swiveled his chair so that his feet were nowhere near the woman's head. She, for her part, moved closer to the railing, and looked at him with terror.

"Are we far enough out to be safe for the moment?" Bogle asked.

"Yes, sir," Lee said. "At this distance it will take the wave almost a day to reach us. And its intensity will have decreased by almost fifty percent."

"All stop," Bogle said. He got out of his chair, and stepped past three survivors. They gathered their legs up close, and watched him as if he were some lumbering giant—which, from their perspective, he probably was.

He stopped beside Lee, who was again looking into his scope.

"Do you know what happened?"

"They've gone to full impulse power," Lee said. "It seems they're trying to outrun the wave."

"They can't do that at impulse," Bogle said. "Why didn't they jump to warp?"

"Maybe something broke down," Lee said, glancing up at the captain. "It does happen, and usually at the worst times. And their ship took quite a beating doing that rescue operation."

Bogle nodded. That would seem more logical. Kirk might take risks that Bogle didn't agree with, but he never seemed to take unreasonable risks.

At least, not with people's lives.

With people's careers, maybe, but not their lives.

"How long do they have?" Bogle asked.

"Ten seconds to impact," Lee said.

Ten seconds.

Ten seconds wasn't even long enough to make a decision, let alone figure out a way to assist them.

Come on, Jim.

He didn't dare die now. Bogle didn't think he

could be nearly as convincing as Kirk in discussing the reasons behind all the Tautean survivors aboard.

Besides, if the *Enterprise* was destroyed, the fleet would lose one of its best ships.

"Sir, they're powering up photon torpedoes."

Bogle laughed in spite of the situation. "Kirk just won't say die. He's going to blast a hole in the wave."

Lee stood, but kept his face pressed to the scope. "They fired ten torpedoes at point-blank range!"

"Well?" Bogle said, almost fearing the news. "Did they make it?"

Lee didn't respond. He shifted from foot to foot, staring into the screen.

The rest of the bridge crew leaned forward.

The survivors merely looked confused.

Bogle resisted the urge to rub his hands together nervously.

This last was one strain too many in an unbelievable day. The second time they had stood on the sidelines and watched the *Enterprise* in a scrape.

Come on, Jim.

Finally Lee straightened away from the scope. He was grinning.

"The wave is past them," he said. "They seem dead in space, but they are still in one piece."

"Yessss!" Bogle said, clenching a fist and shaking it. The rest of the crew grinned too. Bogle cleared his throat, tugged his shirt into place, and resumed his dignified-captain pose as if he hadn't just acted like a schoolboy whose team had won the championship.

"Hail the *Enterprise,* Gustavus."

"Aye, sir," she said. She moved her hand across the communications board. "I'm getting no response."

"Two Klingon vessels are dropping out of warp near us, sir," Rodriguez said.

Bogle turned to Lee. "Can we get back to the *Enterprise?*"

Lee shook his head. "No, sir, not for a few days at least. They're inside that expanding sphere of the subspace wave. The same thing would happen to us if we tried to go back that just happened to them. We have to wait until the intensity of the wave has diminished by a factor of fifty at least."

"We're being hailed by the Klingons," Gustavus said.

"On screen," Bogle said. He turned, narrowly missing the feet of a Tauteean infant. The child squalled and crawled back toward its mother.

Bogle barely managed to face the screen before KerDaq's image appeared.

"It seems your friend Kirk has gotten himself in trouble again," KerDaq said.

Bogle nodded. "It seems that way."

"Are you foolish enough to try to return?" KerDaq asked.

"There is nothing we can do at the moment," Bogle said. "We need to proceed to the starbase and unload these survivors."

"I agree," KerDaq said. "Then we shall return to help Kirk."

" 'We'?" Bogle blurted out the word in spite of himself. He couldn't really believe what he had just heard. But he was facing a Klingon who was temporarily his ally. He should have been more tactful.

KerDaq snorted. "Kirk saved my life when the wave smashed my ship. Returning is the honorable thing to do."

It was, but Bogle hadn't realized the Klingons would feel that way. There was so little that he really knew about them. "We'll rendezvous after we drop off the survivors on Starbase Eleven," Bogle said.

"I shall leave you a time and place," KerDaq said. His image winked off the screen.

"I was supposed to say that," Bogle muttered. But it didn't matter. They had agreed. And if KerDaq understood the word "honor" the way Bogle did, they would set up a rendezvous and return for the *Enterprise*.

"Mr. Rodriguez," Bogle said. "Full speed to Starbase Eleven. Engage when ready."

Then Bogle returned to his chair and sank into it heavily. Lee stepped past a group of survivors to stand beside Bogle. "Well, Mister Lee," Bogle said, "when Kirk's involved, the universe is never a dull place."

Lee laughed. "I think that's an understatement, Captain."

"You know, Mr. Lee," Bogle said, smiling to himself, "I believe you're right."

Chapter Thirty-Three

PRESCOTT WAS TUCKED under the console, her knees against her chin and her arms trapped at her sides. She had braced herself as well as she could, but even that was not well enough. She was nauseated and terrified and angry at herself for the first two emotions, and for causing this mess in the first place.

The ship was rocking like a Tauteean Silksail in a hurricane. People were being tossed all over the ship. Lieutenant Uhura fell against Prescott's console. Mister Sulu tumbled off his chair. Mister Chekov flew through the air like a ball thrown by a child.

Only Mister Spock held his ground, as if by magic.

The clang and clatter was terrifying, and beneath

it was the rumble of the ship herself, as if she were screaming in protest.

Even the moon's breakup had not been this violent. They had said this would be worse, but she hadn't imagined anything this bad. Apparently her imagination hadn't been good enough.

Then Captain James Kirk flew out of his chair. He looked graceful for a moment, tumbling feet over forehead, as if he had intended to fall all along. The illusion was shattered, though, when he slammed into Mister Chekov's console. He brought a hand up, moaned, and collapsed.

The shaking stopped.

All except the shaking inside.

Lieutenant Uhura stood first. She staggered as if she couldn't quite get her balance, then made her way back to her chair. Mister Chekov moaned and grabbed his arm. Mister Spock helped one of the crewmen out from under a nearby console.

No one, apparently, had noticed Captain James Kirk.

Prescott crawled quickly on hands and knees under the rail and down to where Captain James Kirk lay sprawled beside the navigation console. He had a massive cut along the top of his head which seemed to be bleeding a river of dark red blood.

Mister Chekov, still clutching his arm, hurried down the stairs beside her. He knelt near the console, let go of his arm, and pressed his hand against Captain James Kirk's neck.

"He's alive," Mister Chekov said. "But I don't know for how long."

Mister Sulu punched a comm-link button while Prescott and Mister Chekov worked to stop the blood from flowing. "Dr. McCoy to the bridge," Mister Sulu said.

Behind her Prescott heard Spock say, "Mister Scott, I need a status report." Obviously this crew was well trained. Even with their leader injured, they went on.

Captain James Kirk moaned, but didn't regain consciousness. She carefully eased his head into her lap and used her sleeve to stop the blood flow from the gash on his head. She had reached an understanding with this man. They had communicated one leader to another. He had helped her. She would be able to move forward because of him.

He couldn't die.

Not here, not now.

Not after they'd been through so much.

Mister Sulu dropped down beside them with what appeared to be a device similar to the one Dr. Leonard McCoy used. Mister Sulu ran it quickly over Captain James Kirk, then used another setting on the device to stop the blood flow. The cut stopped bleeding and then closed as if by miracle.

Then Mister Sulu turned to Spock. "He's got a slight concussion. I don't know how serious it is, but he'll live." Then Mister Sulu smiled. "I'm just glad I'm not going to have the headache."

Prescott felt relief run through her. These people were like magicians. Their technology was so advanced that it was beyond her. Everything they did was a miracle.

Including saving their leader as if his injury were

routine instead of life-threatening. A Tauteean who had suffered that much blood loss away from a medical facility would probably have died.

"Return to your posts," Spock said. "I need a ship's status report, since Mister Scott is not responding."

Just then the comm line buzzed. "Scott to bridge."

"Go ahead, Mister Scott," Spock said. Prescott marveled at the man's calm even in the face of this disaster. Didn't he have any emotions?

"The old girl took quite a pounding, Mister Spock," Mister Scott said. Mister Scott's voice sounded excited and he seemed winded. "All engines are off-line and will be for some time. She's suffered so much damage, I doubt I can fix her in a week. But she made it, Mister Spock. She survived just fine. She's a marvelous lassie, she is."

"Yes, she is," Spock said dryly, as if he were humoring Mister Scott. "What is the status of life-support? Our bridge lights are still dim."

"Well, sir, the bridge lights and life-support are two separate systems, even though they're part of the environmental controls."

"I realize this, Mister Scott," Spock said. "That is why I specifically asked about life-support."

"All decks have full life-support," Mister Scott said, as if it were obvious. Prescott grinned, and put her head down so that no one could see her. "And structurally the *Enterprise* is fine. We're just stuck here for a while."

"Thank you, Mister Scott," Spock said. He

punched the intercom button as if it had annoyed him.

That was the first hint of emotion that Prescott had seen him display.

"It seems," Spock said, turning and glancing down at Captain James Kirk in Prescott's arms, "that we beat the odds again."

Prescott looked up at Spock. "I think beating the odds would be an understatement for me and my people."

Spock's eyebrow lifted, as he were actually calculating the odds she had just mentioned. For all she knew, he was.

She didn't want to know what they were.

And she wasn't sure she ever wanted to.

Chapter Thirty-four

THE BLACKNESS SLOWLY EASED, replaced by light and a stabbing pain in the side of his head.

Kirk moaned, then blinked—or attempted to. His eyes felt gummed shut.

His ribs ached. He was still sprawled on the deck—he recognized its hardness against his back—but someone was holding his head. Cradling it, in fact. The fingers on the side of his face were as light as feathers.

He wanted to stay in the darkness, but he couldn't. He had things to do. He couldn't quite remember what, but he knew he would when he opened his eyes.

He moaned again, and blinked. This time his eyelids fluttered.

Blurry faces hovered above him, and behind them light. Painful light.

He blinked again and his eyes focused on Prescott's tiny features. She smiled. "Welcome back, Captain James Kirk."

"About time you woke up." McCoy's loud, grating voice seemed to echo around the pain inside his head.

"Ow," Kirk said.

McCoy laughed. That sound was even more unpleasant than his voice. Why hadn't Kirk noticed that before?

"The headache will go away shortly," McCoy said.

"Could you please lower your voice, Doctor?" Kirk asked.

Above him Prescott laughed. Maybe the doctor hadn't really been talking that loud.

The headache receded a bit. The rest of his memory gathered together. He remembered the subspace wave. "Am I the only one who was injured?" he asked.

"I wish," McCoy said.

Kirk pushed himself into a sitting position with the help of Prescott. "The wave. Did it damage the ship?"

He barely got the words out before the room spun and he had to close his eyes against the pain. Then, after a moment it eased and he opened them again. Now the room was only spinning slowly. And as he focused, it stopped.

He had been lying on the floor near the navigation station. Prescott was sitting beside him, and McCoy knelt above him.

"We survived the wave, Captain," Spock said from somewhere beyond Kirk's range of vision.

"Well, if he's asking about the ship, he's fine," McCoy said. He peered at Kirk. "I have about five hundred patients who need me and it's clear you don't anymore." He stood and headed for the lift door. He stopped just inside and stuck his head back out. "Captain, I'd tell you to report to sickbay, but I don't have room for you. And I'd tell you to rest in your quarters, but we don't have room for you there either. So against doctor's best judgment, you can stay on duty."

McCoy stepped back and the turbolift doors whooshed closed over the sound of light laughter.

Prescott and Sulu both helped Kirk to his feet and to his command chair. Sitting on the hard padding hurt even worse this time. He had to have bruises over half his body.

"How long was I out?" he asked, bringing a hand to his forehead. A lump had grown there.

"About an hour, sir," Sulu said. "It took Dr. McCoy that long to reach the bridge."

Kirk raised his head gingerly. He remembered the tossing and bucking.

Barely.

"Is it that bad below?"

Sulu nodded. "Yes, sir."

Kirk forced himself to take two deep breaths, then swiveled slowly to face Spock. Might as well get back to work.

Doctor's orders.

"What's our status, Mister Spock?"

Spock nodded at him, and Kirk thought he saw the ghost of a smile flit across Spock's lips. Then Spock clasped his hands behind his back and looked as serious as ever. "Life-support is fully functional, Captain. The hull came through the event without major damage. All shields are at forty percent. Both the warp engines and impulse power are off-line."

"For how long?"

"To quote Chief Engineer Scott, sir, 'We ain't going nowhere fast.' I believe those were his exact words."

For a moment Kirk couldn't believe what he had just heard. Then he started laughing. "I would hope so, Mr. Spock."

And the rest of the bridge crew laughed too. Their laughter made Kirk laugh harder. And the more he laughed, the more his head hurt. But it was a good hurt this time.

Captain's log, supplemental

The *Enterprise* has remained in this position for almost two days while Chief Engineer Scott and his crew effect repairs. The ship was damaged in a huge subspace wave created when the *Enterprise,* the *Farragut,* and two Klingon vessels destroyed the rift in the Tautee system.

The Klingons, led by KerDaq, rescued survivors of the Tautee disaster and, following the suggestion of Captain Kelly Bogle of the *U.S.S. Farragut,* took them to Starbase 11. Then the Klingon ships and the *Farragut,* now empty, returned to the *Enterprise.*

Bogle tells me this was KerDaq's idea. If I had heard that from anyone but Bogle, I would think it hyperbole. But Bogle does not exaggerate, especially when it comes to Klingons.

I do not expect a friendly interaction with KerDaq, but I am surprised at the amount of courtesy the Klingons have shown so far. If this incident is any indication of the future, the Federation and the Klingons may well be able to work together someday.

The damage sustained during that last wave affected the warp engines most severely. Chief Engineer Scott is working to bring the warp drive back up on-line. The *Farragut*'s science officer, Richard Lee, is assisting in the final stages of getting the warp drive on-line. I am also transferring half the Tauteean refugees to the *Farragut* to give us more room on the return to Starbase 11.

Between the four ships, we managed to rescue over two thousand survivors. Most of those beamed up to the *Enterprise* were wounded. Several more were injured in the impact with the final subspace wave. It should be noted that Dr. Leonard McCoy and his staff have done an outstanding job over the last forty-eight hours. Working in primitive conditions, with limited resources, McCoy and his team saved almost every life in their care. I recommend that a special commendation be attached to McCoy's file.

Prescott, the leader of one group of Tauteean survivors, was instrumental in helping us close the rift in space. She and the remaining Tautee survivors will be treated on Starbase 11 and then will be sent with supplies and Federation personnel to settle a new world. I expect in a few hundred years the Tauteeans will be full and proud members of the Federation.

"Captain." Uhura's voice broke through Kirk's concentration on his log. He punched the Off button and turned to her.

She sat in her usual position, hand to her ear, legs tucked behind her chair. Her eyes were wide, as if the message had startled her. "KerDaq is hailing you."

"Put it on screen," Kirk said. He swiveled his chair so that he faced the screen directly.

KerDaq sat in his own command chair, arms crossed, steel bracelets glinting in the odd green light. "Kirk, I see you have found a way to survive yet again."

Kirk laughed. "I do my best." Then he let the smile ease off his face. He had to handle this next carefully. But he had to say it, even if he did not know the Klingon way. "I am glad that you returned to help us. Thank you."

KerDaq spit in disgust on the floor. "You saved my crew when the subspace wave destroyed our ship. I did not return out of kindness. I owed you, Kirk. Now the debt is paid." He smiled "Besides, I would not give you the honor of dying to save thousands. Only a Klingon deserves such honor."

"Understood," Kirk said, smiling.

KerDaq smiled, too.

Prescott stepped forward beside Kirk and looked up for permission to speak. He glanced at her and nodded.

"KerDaq," Prescott said, "my people thank you, too."

KerDaq leaned forward until his face filled the screen. "You are sentimental fools. You will fit well with the Federation. It too is full of sentimental fools."

Then the screen went dark.

"He cut off communication, sir," Uhura said.

"I gathered that, Lieutenant."

The screen flickered back to life to show the two Klingon cruisers turning and jumping to warp.

"What did I say wrong?" Prescott said. "I hope I didn't—"

Kirk laughed and touched her thin, frail shoulder. "You did nothing wrong. It was just the Klingon way of saying, 'You're welcome.'"

Prescott shook her head. "This is a strange universe we live in. It will take some getting used to it."

"Yes," Kirk said, dropping down into his chair. "Yes, it will."

Epilogue

THE CARGO HOLD would never be the same for McCoy and he half wished he'd never have to return to it. The Tauteean survivors had been off the *Enterprise* now for three days and the ship had been undergoing repairs at Starbase Eleven. And he had been spending most of the last three days working on the Starbase with the medical staff, tending to what seemed to be thousands of wounded survivors. He hadn't realized he could be so tired and still move. Somehow his body wasn't quite ready to rest yet.

As he approached the cargo bay he could hear laughing. The last time he'd been in this corridor it had been littered with the injured survivors. He tried to force that picture out of his mind, but didn't have much luck.

That picture would be with him for a long, long time.

The door to the cargo bay were locked open in front of him and he stepped inside. Since the survivors had left, the bay had been cleaned and he couldn't even tell it had been used for a huge sickbay just a few short days before. There was no blood and no smell of rotting flesh.

No injured bodies.

No ruined legs.

No gangrene.

The cargo bay as it had been before McCoy had even heard of Tautee.

A large monitor was in place between two huge machines again and an ensign wore the helmet. Scotty had his projectors working again. And it looked as if, even with all the time spent getting the *Enterprise* back in shape, he'd also managed to find the time to get his projectors working right. How that man did it, McCoy would never know.

"Come in, Doctor," Kirk yelled from across the bay, smiling and motioning for McCoy to join the party. "We're celebrating a mission well-completed."

"Actually, Captain," Spock said from a position halfway between Kirk and McCoy, "there are still many items of business that must be attended to."

Kirk waved Spock's statement away. "Mister Spock, there must always be a point where a mission is declared finished."

Spock frowned, obviously from the illogic of Kirk's statement and McCoy found his spirits suddenly starting to lift. Anything that would annoy Mister Spock and break through that stone-like exterior was fine by him.

About twenty people filled the area where the cargo deck left off and Scotty's huge machines took up. Sulu and Chekov were laughing about something with two women ensigns from the starbase. Scotty was complaining about a table someone had set too close to one of his machines. On the table sat a large cake and a vast supply of wine. Someone had spared no expense for this party, that was for sure.

Kirk was standing near the table. He laughed at Spock's reaction, then turned back to a discussion he had obviously been having with Captain Bogle of the *Farragut*. McCoy was amazed Bogle was even speaking to Kirk after Kirk dumped all those extra survivors on him. Kirk and Bogle had exchanged harsh words about gambling with lives and being too caught up in rules. But Admiral Hoffman had pointed out that both sides were important.

And had to work together.

Then she had settled it all by siding with Kirk on the Prime Directive issue, but giving Bogle a commendation for staying within Starfleet guidelines.

So both men shook hands, buried the hatchet and participated in all other clichés. Then they had played an all-night game of poker, with Kirk bluffing and Bogle playing strictly by the rules.

Then, from what McCoy understood, Bogle had gone in the next day and asked to be assigned to the vacant seat on Starfleet's Plans and Policy commission. If his transfer was accepted, McCoy knew Bogle would work hard to tighten up the Prime

Directive. In fact, McCoy bet that after this incident, it would be Bogle's main focus. Who knew how tight the rule would be in eighty or so years.

But, for the moment, Kirk and Bogle seemed to be friends again. As much as those two very different men could be friends.

McCoy had heard all of this while he had been working with the survivors. If he never saw an infected wound again he would be extremely happy. He was glad that the starbases had more medical personnel than a starship, or else he would never have gotten any sleep.

But the most important thing was that the Tauteean race survived with enough people to start over on a new planet.

McCoy took a drink offered by the science officer of the *Farragut,* Mister Lee.

"Mister Spock," Scotty said, loud enough for everyone to hear. "How would you like to be the very first to try my new course?"

"Golf is not a logical game, Mister Scott," Spock said.

"It is if you're from Scotland, laddy," Scott said and everyone laughed.

For a moment the buzz of conversation filled the cargo deck. McCoy moved over to where Chief Engineer Scott stood beside one of his machines like a father watching over a young child.

"Doctor," Scotty said. "What do ya think now?" He waved his hand at the beautiful green showing on the monitor. There were even a few white clouds floating in the deep blue sky.

"Wonderful," McCoy said, really meaning it. "But how'd you get it to work?"

Scotty pointed to a brown-haired man standing twenty feet away beside the other projector. "Mister Projeff Ellis, the chief engineer of the *Farragut,* helped me. With him on one machine and me on the other, we got the lassies to finally balance. And ya know, he agrees that someday this might be possible without a helmet."

"Great," McCoy said, staring at the monitor full of an expanse of green grass and trees and blue sky. Maybe Scotty had a point. Maybe this new invention would be good to have around. As long as people didn't take it too seriously.

"And you know, Doctor," Scott went on. "Projeff loves golf as much as I do. Says he plays every time he gets a chance. He must have Scotsman in his blood."

"That he must, Scotty," McCoy said.

"All right, everyone," Kirk's voice drowned out the background buzz of talking and laughing. "It's time for a toast." He held up his glass and waited until everyone found one and was quiet.

Lieutenant Uhura handed McCoy a fresh glass of wine and McCoy held it aloft, waiting for the toast.

"To Captain Bogle and his fine crew," Kirk said, his voice ringing through the room. "To my wonderful crew. To the Klingons for helping. And most of all to the Tauteean survivors. May they flourish in their new home."

With that he and Captain Bogle touched glasses and drank.

"Hear! Hear!" the crowd shouted, raising their glasses together in toast.

With that sip of smooth-tasting wine, McCoy could feel the ghosts of the injured and dead survivors being pushed back into the past where they belonged. He could feel his body relaxing and the exhaustion creeping up. Billions of lives had been lost in the Tautee system, but somehow, he found a sense of fulfillment in the fact that the *Enterprise,* the *Farragut,* and the Klingon ships had saved enough lives for the Tautee race to continue. He felt good that he was a part of such a rescue.

But it was now time to do as Scotty had done with the cargo bay. McCoy had to clear the decks and move on. Besides, he had a medical experiment he needed to finish. Right after he took a very long nap.

McCoy glanced out over at the golf course on the monitor between the machines. What a peaceful place it seemed. He felt as if he wanted to just walk out there and keep walking. Maybe, when he took his next leave, he'd play a round of golf.

"Now," Kirk said, his voice carrying over the talking. "I expect this party to last all night."

Spock gave the captain a sour look and McCoy laughed. The longer it lasted, the better. That sounded perfect. Even Spock's doleful expression was perfect.

Especially Spock's doleful expression.

McCoy grinned. This was the best party he could remember attending in a long, long time.

When Dean Wesley Smith and Kristine Kathryn Rusch met at a writing workshop in New Mexico, they already had a few publishing credentials to their names. Dean had sold over a hundred poems and short stories to *The Twilight Zone, Night Cry,* and *Writers of the Future,* Vol. 1. Kris had sold more nonfiction than she could count and stories to *Aboriginal SF* and *Amazing Stories.* Their writing careers flourished after their romance started. Dean has sold over sixty short stories and seven novels, including *Carnage in New York* and *Laying the Music to Rest.* Kris doesn't count the short-story sales any more than she counted the nonfiction, but she has sold eleven novels. The most recent are *The Fey: Sacrifice* (Bantam) and *The Devil's Churn* (Dell).

Dean and Kris collaborated on a publishing company, Pulphouse Publishing. That joint venture has brought them one World Fantasy Award, another nomination, a Hugo nomination, and a house full of books (including numerous copies of *The Best of Pulphouse,* from St. Martin's Press). Kris has stopped editing for Pulphouse, and now edits *The Magazine of Fantasy and Science Fiction* (for which she won the Hugo award in 1994). Dean publishes all the Pulphouse products and edits *Pulphouse: A Fiction Magazine.*

In 1991, they started to collaborate on fiction. "Model Lover," their first attempt, appeared in *Ghosttide.* Another collaborative story appeared in the *Twilight Zone Anthology* from DAW. Their most recent collaboration is in the *Star Trek: Deep Space Nine* series: *The Long Night.* Pocket Books also published their collaborative novels *The Escape* (in the *Voyager* series) and, under the pen name Sandy Schofield, *The Big Game* (in the *Deep Space Nine* series). They, under their own names and under Sandy's name, have several more novels in the works.

STAR TREK®
PHASE II
THE LOST SERIES

Judith and Garfield Reeves-Stevens

STAR TREK PHASE II: THE LOST SERIES is the story of the missing chapter in the STAR TREK saga. The series, set to start production in 1977, would have reunited all of the original cast except Leonard Nimoy. However, Paramount Pictures decided to shift gears to feature film production, shutting down the television series. Full of never-before-seen color artwork, storyboards, blueprints, technical information and photos, this book reveals the vision behind Gene Roddenberry's lost glimpse of the future.

POCKET
B O O K S

Coming in mid-August in Hardcover
from Pocket Books

FIRST TIME IN PRINT!

STAR TREK®
STARFLEET ACADEMY®

The first adventures of cadets James T. Kirk, Leonard McCoy and the Vulcan Spock!

From Spock's momentous decision to attend Starfleet Academy on Earth, through his first meeting with the medical student McCoy and their action-packed adventure with the ultra-serious, ultra-daring Cadet Kirk, these illustrated adventures will take readers "where no one has gone before"™—back to the very beginning!

1 CRISIS ON VULCAN
By Brad and Barbara Strickland
(coming in mid-July 1996)

2 AFTERSHOCK
By John Vornholt
(mid-August 1996)

3 CADET KIRK
By Diane L. Carey
(mid-September 1996)

Available wherever STAR TREK books are sold!

A MINSTREL® BOOK
Published by Pocket Books

1207